PERILOUS LAST-CHRISTMAS SHOPPING

A CHILLING PSYCHOLOGICAL THRILLER

ANNIE DE MUYNCK

www.dizzyemupublishing.com

DIZZY EMU PUBLISHING

1714 N McCadden Place, Hollywood, Los Angeles 90028

www.dizzyemupublishing.com

Perilous Last-Minute Christmas Shopping

A Chilling Psychological Thriller

Annie De Muynck

ISBN: 9798689203591

First published in the United States

in 2020 by Dizzy Emu Publishing

www.dizzyemupublishing.com

ABOUT THE AUTHOR

Annie De Muynck (nickname Anne) has a long career as a psychologist in a guidance center. After University she specialized in psychoanalytic counselling. In addition she has worked as a free-lance translator for English and American clients. She followed writers and screenwriters classes in London. She was a member of London and Medway Writers and Film groups. Her native is Belgium and she lived part time in England and France.

ALSO BY ANNIE DE MUYNCK

Non-fiction:

NYT 2017 best-selling hot new release screenplay Book Series She Has No Choice Part One, Part Two and Part Three. Dizzy Emu Publishing and Amazon.

Academic:

Speaker at the International Congress 12-15 May 1995, University Ghent, Freud's Pre-Analytical Writings (1877-1900) with paper and subject Aphasia and Memory: Autour de "Zum psychischen Mechanismus der Vergesslichkeit (1898)"
Papers published in the periodical "Rondzendbrief uit het Freudiaanse veld".

ACKNOWLEDGEMENTS

Thanks to Euroscript Ltd. London and London Screenwriters' Festival. Thanks to all the people and friends from the Euroscript Development Workshops and the London Writers' groups who gave me feedback and support. Because of you my learning curve accelerated in storytelling, genre and dark writing, character development, visual writing, dialogue writing etc.

Thanks to the publishers.

PART ONE

CHAPTER ONE

Christmas decorations hang liberally and themed carols feed the atmosphere in the open plan kitchen. The dining table is in all its glory. Plentiful of food in the kitchen, on the cooker and in the oven. Chrissie, an attractive twenty-something brunette sits on the couch with a laptop. She wears a fashionable jacket, a woollen hat, scarf and slippers. Her mother Doreen prepares the Christmas Eve supper. Chrissie finishes her work on a spreadsheet while she talks with her office via the phone.

"Done," says Chrissie.

Chrissie closes off the laptop and talks to her colleague.

"Look, I really have to dash off. Yes, I'll see what I can do on boxing day. See you after the holidays. Happy Christmas!"

She puts the mobile in her handbag. She walks towards the Christmas tree for a last look.

"Make sure you're back before your sister and the children arrive," says Doreen.

Chrissie admires the table.

"The table looks fabulous!"

Chrissie puts on her old boots.

"Don't forget to buy yourself a new pair of boots. Very good idea that clothing voucher your sister gave you ahead of Christmas," says Doreen.

Doreen burns her hand at the stove and withdraws her hand.

"Ouch!"

"Watch out! I'm sorry I can't help you any longer. The office is manic," says Chrissie.

"You better hurry before the shops close. It's last minute Christmas shopping Chrissie."

"Most of my gifts are already under the tree. I only need to buy a few more," answers Chrissie.

Chrissie takes her handbag and wants to leave the room.

"I wonder how you'll ever find time for your own family with that job. That must be the reason you split up with Jake," continues Doreen.

"Mum let's not talk about that during the holidays. Remember my New Year's resolutions. My own flat!"

Doreen sighs. Chrissie leaves the room.

Twenty minutes later Chrissie leaves the underground. The sun shines. She walks into a busy London Christmas shopping street and enters a shopping mall.

It's dark outside. Chrissie walks in a quiet street. She's packed with bags. In one of the bags are a few wrapped bottles. Chrissie sighs. She looks around and heads for a small park. She wears the new pair of boots. She stops and tinkers at one of her boots.

Chrissie enters a small park and heads for a bench. She places the bags on the bench. She takes off a boot and arranges her nylon sock. She rubs painfully over her foot.

"Ouch!"

While she puts on the boot again, a signal on her smart phone sounds. She checks the message. Suddenly a Santa Claus appears behind her. He snatches her handbag and one of her shopping bags. He runs. Chrissie immediately picks up the other bags and follows the man.

"Hey! Hey!"

The Santa runs fast. Chrissie breaks the heel of one of her new boots. Her mobile falls on the ground and the battery flops out.

"Damn!"

Fast she takes up the pieces and continues. She can't follow the man and he disappears. She gives up and sits down on a bench.

"Damn!"

She browses her bags and pulls out the old pair of boots. She puts on the old boots. She puts away the new boots with the broken heel.

The Santa arrives in a quiet street. He opens the door of his van and takes off his Santa Claus clothes. He's middle aged and sloppy dressed. He hides the Santa clothes and the stolen bag in the van. He enters the van. He keeps an eye on the park entrance.

Chrissie, still in the park, wants to dial the police but the mobile phone doesn't function. She stands and pushes with one foot against the bench while trying to start up the mobile again. It starts to rain. She looks at the sky.

"Oh no!"

She picks up the bags and walks outside the park. She hides the mobile in her jacket pocket.

More rain. She runs towards a shop to shelter from the rain. However the shutters close. She has to pull back. She notices a pub and browses her pocket. She finds a coin. She takes it out and inspects the coin, it's a two pound coin. When she arrives at the pub the shutters are already down. She sighs. She's wet and shivers. She looks around. She finds no shelter from the rain. When she arrives at the van, in the quiet street, the former Santa Claus, pops out. She does not recognize her mugger and she interrupts him.

"Excuse me, could I use your mobile?"

"Why?"

"My handbag was stolen. I want to call the police."

The man enters the filthy van and makes a gesture that she must enter the van.

"I don't want my mobile wet. Do sit down."

She hesitates and shivers again. She looks around and sees no one else to ask, only more rain.

Chrissie sits down with one foot outside the van.

"Do close the door. It's cold," says the man.

Chrissie puts the door ajar, still one foot half outside. He hands over his mobile. She anxiously tries the mobile but it doesn't work.

"Hey, it doesn't work."

The man sighs. He takes the mobile and examines.

"Sorry about that. I've to top up. I'll drop you at the police station. It's on my way. Do close the door!"

Very suddenly he starts the engine.

"Wait, wait!"

Chrissie can't but close the door. Santa Claus locks the doors.

"Stop! Stop! Let me out! Let me walk to the police station."

"No worries. I'll drop you."

The man drives fast. The street is deserted. Chrissie sits as frozen. The driver ignores when a red light pops up and continues.

"Hey, that was a red light!"

The man lays his hand on her arm gently.

"No worries. Why is it that you're alone on a Christmas eve?"

"Last minute shopping."

"What presents do you have? Let me have a look."

The man browses her bag. She withdraws her bags. The man uses both hands again for steering and starts driving faster in the wrong direction.

Chrissie looks around. She's very pale and upset.

"Why do you take that direction?"

"You're in safe hands."

Chrissie is quiet. She looks around. She notices in the back of the van, a red piece of cloth that belongs to the Santa Claus disguise.

"Do stop the car. Let me out!"

The man turns on the music and lays his hand on her leg. She pulls away.

She withdraws as far as possible.

They drive on a highway surrounded by countryside.

Santa browses the bags again and finds chocolates and four wrapped bottles of wine.

"I'm thirsty."

Santa browses Chrissie's bags again and finds chocolates and four wrapped bottles of wine.

"There is enough for a party!"

He takes out one bottle and unwraps it fast with one hand. The car makes a wrong move while doing that. He gains control of the van again.

"Would you be so kind to open it for me?"

When Chrissie doesn't react immediately. He places the bottle on her legs.

"I'm driving, you know. Can't do everything!"

Chrissie opens the bottle and hands it over to the man. He drinks.

"Do stop here. I want to get out."

He places the bottle between his legs and lays his hand on her leg again.

"Not in the mood for a bit of fun?"

She pushes his arm away hysterical.

"Ooooh! The lady's angry!"

"Do stop the car now!"

He lessens speed and stops the car. She opens the door and jumps out grabbing her bags. He snatches another bottle before letting her go.

"Let me have at least a decent drink on Christmas eve darling."

She slams the door. The van disappears with a lot of noise. Chrissie looks around dumbfounded. She notices the woodland. However another trucker trumpets with flashing lights on her.

"Aaah!"

Frightened, she jumps over the low highway fence and runs away in the field, as fast as she can. The trucker stops and keeps flashing and trumpeting.

She runs and runs in the wet field without looking back. It doesn't rain but there's mud. The trucker, an older dark man, leaves his truck.

"Hey hey, darling come back, you'll get lost! I'll bring you home!"

She looks over her shoulder and hesitates. The Santa has turned around his van and drives now high speed in the direction of the trucker and the potential rescuer of Chrissie. The trucker has a narrow escape from the van of the abductor and enters quickly his truck again. Chrissie runs into the direction of the woodland. She disappears in the wood.

She runs and runs. She's exhausted from running and breathes heavily. She stumbles by times. After a while Chrissie arrives at a field.

She looks around bewildered.

"Where am I?"

She inspects the surroundings and can't see any sign of life, no lights, no sound. She leans against a lonely tree and breathes heavily. She takes her mobile. It doesn't react. After a while she walks again, further away from the wood. She covers her ears with her hand while she looks around. She walks and walks. She notices a railway. Chrissie looks up when there is noise of an arriving train. She runs towards the rails and waves with both her arms.

"Stop, stop!"

The train disappears again.

"Ooooh!"

She lets her head sink. She takes a bottle of wine out of her bag. She unwraps the bottle and drinks after opening the bottle. She closes the bottle. She continues walking but less fast, the bottle in her hand. She stumbles by times. She walks away from the railway. She notices an old wooden hovel, surrounded by some trees. She heads for it. She walks around the cabin and opens the door.

Chrissie sits on the hay inside the hovel and drinks more wine. She unwraps a bar of chocolates and eats some. She lies down and falls asleep instantly.

CHAPTER TWO

It is Christmas day, early morning, dawn. Joe, a tall middle aged man in very rough clothes, walks towards a wooden armchair inside his dark carpenter's workroom in the country. On the armchair sits the decayed body of a young woman, Katie, wrapped in a large plastic translucent bag.

Once outside in the courtyard Joe lays Katie on a horse-drawn carriage and covers the body in the plastic bag with a dirty blanket. The horse-drawn carriage stands before the small side-building with two windows, the workroom. It is situated between an old house and a stable for the horse and the outside loo. The old house has four windows with a view on the large courtyard. Everything is walled in. Joe opens the large wooden gates of the courtyard outwards. He unties the horse and climbs on the carriage. He takes the horse reins. He hits the horse. The horse moves. Joe drives horse and carriage outside. He climbs down, closes and locks the wooden gates.

Joe arrives at the hovel-cabin where Chrissie is still asleep. He enters the hovel. He looks surprised to find a girl asleep. Joe shouts.
"Hey!"

She doesn't awakens. He takes her up and walks towards the door, carrying Chrissie. With his foot he opens the door. He lays Chrissie on the carriage and takes off the decayed body, Katie. He goes inside the hovel with Katie. When he's back he loads Chrissie's bags also on the carriage. He unties the horse and climbs on the carriage. He takes the horse reins. He hits the horse. The horse moves.

"Juuuu!"

They leave.

It's a cold and sunny winter day. The large wooden gates of the courtyard open outwards. Joe drives horse and carriage inside. Joe climbs down and closes the wooden gates. His middle aged wife, Louise, stands outside the house. She's dressed with simple and dark clothes. The dog barks and runs around the carriage. Some wood panels stand against the wall. Carpenter utensils lie on the floor. His son Rick, a tall attractive young man with long blond hair, wearing jeans and a sweater, runs from the side building towards the carriage with Chrissie.

"Wauw! I guess she's a model!"

Rick hangs over Chrissie.

"Ha ha, go away kid," says Joe.

Rick doesn't move. Joe pushes Rick cheerful.

"Away I said."

Louise comes closer and stands next Rick. She touches Rick's arm.

"Who's that? Is she ill?"

Joe explains.

"She seems to be in a deep sleep! We've a new lodger for Christmas. Let's take her to the spare bedroom."

He lifts Chrissie under her arms and talks to Rick.

"Rick, now help me."

Rick's eager to help. He takes her feet and they carry her into the house.

Louise arranges the blankets in the spare bedroom. The room is furnished with wood. A wooden chest with drawers stands opposite the bed. There is no window, but a mirror above the chest. Rick and Joe lay Chrissie on the bed. Joe leaves. Rick picks up the empty water pitcher and leaves also. Louise takes off Chrissie's boots. She looks around and picks up the photo on the chest of a young woman. Katie. She puts it away in the drawer. Rick comes back with Chrissie's bags and the water-pitcher filled with water. He puts the pitcher inside the empty water basin and the bags next to the bed. He peers at the packets in the bags, Chrissie's Christmas presents. He shakes his head. Louise takes a clean towel from the chest and puts it on top of the chest. They leave. Rick casts a covetous eye on Chrissie, before he sets the door ajar.

The living room is full of wooden furniture and plants. Next to one of the two windows, with flower-curtains, are kitchen units with a gas cooker, gas-burner plus water-tank. In the middle stands a round table with six chairs. A stove heats the room. Next to the couches, with flower-cushions, burns the open hearth. Against the wall stands a large book-case and piles of wood for the open hearth and a very simple decorated Christmas tree. Louise cooks breakfast. Rick sits on a couch, the dog sits next him. He plays guitar. Joe comes in and caresses the back of his wife.

"Smells delicious! I'm hungry," says Joe.

Louise replies.

"That young lady might be also. We'll have an even better Christmas meal later!"

"Can't wait, darling!" Joe kisses her neck.

Rick replies.

"What a beautiful girl. And these beautiful presents! I've never seen anything like this. Why is it that we never leave the house?"

"We have a good life here. Outside all dangerous things happen," Joe says. He leaves the room.

"Rick, why do you upset your father always with these questions? You know that your father and I have both endured so much hardship as a child," says Louise.

Rick takes his guitar and starts playing softly. He sings.

"One day I met a beautiful girl. It was like a fairy tale. What a beautiful girl."

In the spare bedroom, Chrissie awakens with a shock. She sits up on the bed. She listens to the noises and the music in the house. She lies again. Then reality kicks in and she sits up again and looks around.

"Where am I?"

She stands and walks towards the door. She stands before the narrow door opening and peers at the living room where Rick sits on the couch and twangs a guitar. Chrissie watches with open mouth. She places both her hands on her head and turns. She walks around the room several times. She notices her packages. She browses and finds her mobile in one of the bags. Frantic she tries the mobile again. No sign. She sits on the bed for a moment with her hand on the bed still holding the mobile. She stares at the wall. She bounces with her head several times on the mattress. Suddenly she stands, puts the mobile in the pocket of her coat and puts on her boots. She walks slowly towards the door again.

The door of the living room is half open. Louise and Rick look up when they notice Chrissie. Rick stops his music and talks to Chrissie.

"Wakey, wakey?"

Chrissie stands still with the door latch in her hands. Louise suddenly approaches Chrissie and takes her arm firmly but gently enough.

"Don't worry. Take a seat. Breakfast is ready. You must be hungry."

They head for the table. Chrissie steps back.

"Where am I?"

"We're in the countryside, darling," explains Louis.

Chrissie walks towards the windows and sees the large inner courtyard. Chrissie opens the door and runs outside.

The dog follows Chrissie outside and barks. She runs immediately at the wooden gate. She tries frantically to open the locks but to no avail. Louise comes outside also. Louise stops Chrissie from progressing with the lock.

"Calm down," urges Louise.

Chrissie pushes Louise away. She bangs with both fists at the wooden gate.

"Let me out of here. I want to go home!"

There is a noise of keys at the other side of the gates. The gates do open outwards. Chrissie wants to run outside. Joe walks inside and immediately guides Chrissie inside and closes the gates again.

"Where are you going? You'll get lost! You're safe here," says Joe.

She steps back terrified. Joe explains more.

"I saved your life, taking you away from that hovel."

"You found me in that hovel?"

"Yes darling. Be our guest!"

He opens his arms and laughs. Chrissie can't but following him, away from the gates.

Chrissie, Rick, Louise and Joe sit at the table in the living room. They just finished breakfast. Chrissie drinks slowly some tea and dreams away. Joe finishes his meal and stands.

"Some work must be done before dark. I'm so looking forward to celebrate Christmas together later," says Joe.

He puts on his boots and leaves the room towards the courtyard. Louise smiles at Chrissie. Chrissie doesn't notice and keeps chewing on a piece of bread. Chrissie lets fall her piece of bread and stands suddenly while pushing her chair away noisily.

"You do not understand!" says Chrissie.

She walks around the table several times. Rick and Louise lean back and stare at Chrissie.

"I have to go back to London immediately."

"That's not possible Chrissie," answers Rick.

Louise helps Rick.

"My husband explained already. The nearest village is really far away and it'll be even colder the next few days. You'll have to wait. We just take care of you!"

Chrissie disagrees.

"Care of me? How in god's name can you all talk like that?"

She looks at both of them. The door opens and Joe comes in again with some plain Christmas presents. Joe walks towards the Christmas tree he arranges them under the tree and talks to Chrissie.

"We'll play musical chairs. What do you think of that, Chrissie?"

"I so enjoyed it last year," says Rick.

Chrissie sinks down on the chair again. Joe picks up a large water can. He talks soft to Louise.

"Louise give me a hand filling the water tank."

Louise helps her husband and Rick goes to the book-case. He talks to Chrissie.

"If you want to read, take one of my books."

She drinks from her cup and looks at Rick. Rick takes one of his old music magazines, sits down at the table and browses the magazine. Rick grabs an apple and bites while reading.

Chrissie walks around in the spare bedroom. She looks in the drawer and finds the photo of a young woman. She holds it up to study it. After a while she places the picture back and opens the chest. She takes out a pullover and trousers and some socks. She pours water in the basin. She washes her face. She looks in the mirror. She sits on the bed. She finds the mobile in the pocket of her coat. Nervously she fiddles the mobile. She opens the device and takes out the battery and sim card. She prudently puts it back in place. Nervously she closes the device again. She pushes a button and shakes the phone. All of a sudden the phone gives a sign of live and starts up.

"Aaach!"

She trembles when she inserts the pin code. Several messages pop up. Chrissie reads mesmerized several messages from her family, that were received on her phone earlier, asking where she is located. She starts texting: Can you track down my location? When she sends, she notices the message fails because there is no connection.

"Oooh!"

She stands and goes over to the other end of the room and tries to make a call but no connection. She lies down on the bed with her mobile in her hand. She switches off the phone totally for saving the battery.

It's evening. The candles on the Christmas tree and on the table lit up the rather dark room. Chrissie is dressed with the spare bedroom pullover and trousers. She sits with the dressed up Joe and Rick at the Christmas table. Joe and Rick wear a Santa Claus hat. They just have finished the meal. Louise clears the table of plates and cutlery. A few wine bottles and filled glasses remain on the table. Rick plays the guitar and Joe taps with his fingers on the table. Joe stands and opens the courtyard door and the dog pops in, a cloth with several blood stains between his teeth. He strokes the dog and takes away the cloth. He flings it in the bin. Joe places three chairs around the Christmas tree.

"Now the presents!"

Chrissie looks up still dumbfounded.

"Don't worry Chrissie, we have a present for you also. We're happy that you're here for Christmas. We all miss Katy," says Rick.

Chrissie asks, "Katie? Who's Katie?!"

Joe takes up a cord with bells and binds it around the middle of the dog.

"Chrissie let's play first. The one who wins gets a present!"

Rick helps his father preparing the dog for the game. Rick walks the dog several times around the room and the bells jingle. Chrissie watches the spectacle amazed. The dog stops and it's silent. Joe and Rick caress and feed the dog. The dog jumps up and barks.

"He remembers well from last year," says Joe.

Joe turns cheerful towards Louise and takes her hand.

"Come here Louise!"

The whole family and Chrissie walk around three chairs and the Christmas tree. The dog walks around the room with the bells. The dog stops and Chrissie sits down fast on a chair. Rick is a second faster than his mum and Louise has lost that game. Joe laughs.

"Haha, you're out darling!"

Joe removes one chair and drinks a few more glasses of wine. He feeds the dog. The dog walks again. They walk around the chairs and tree without Louise now. The dog stops and Chrissie fights with Joe for a chair. Joe howls, like an animal and pushes her away. Chrissie has no chair. Rick laughs.

"Lost! Lost!"

Rick takes a chair away and Joe feeds the dog before another round. Now Joe and Rick fight for the only chair and Joe wins. Rick goes to the tree and takes up a large oblong present.

"That's your present, dad."

Joe opens the present and finds a new saw. He loses every cheerfulness. Joe stands ceremonious and makes the sign of a cross in the air with the saw. He howls again. The dog tries to hide under the table and makes pathetic noises.

"Thanks for that," Joe says.

"It's a superb label. It's the label you used when you worked for that mortician," says Rick.

"It's beyond my expectation," Joe replies.

Joe walks around cheerful again with the saw. Rick adds another chair and he strokes the dog and drags him in the right place for another round.

"More presents to come," says Rick.

After finishing a round Rick goes to the tree and gives another large oblong packet to his mother. He kisses her.

"Happy Christmas! Dad and I made this for you!"

Louise opens the present and the box inside. She finds the skeleton of a small crocodile in wood.

"Thanks. Nice carving. Well done to you both! Something for in our bedroom! "

Joe kisses his wife.

"Haha darling. I like your sense of humour."

Rick and Chrissie now circle one chair and the dog. Rick and Chrissie fight for a chair and Rick laughs, but Chrissie wins. Rick goes again to the tree. He takes another present.

"Now Chrissie's present."

He gives it to Chrissie. Chrissie sits speechless with the packet.

"Do open it," says Rick.

"Thank you."

Chrissie opens the package and finds a jigsaw with title "HIDDEN HIDEAWAY". Rick takes his guitar.

"I even wrote a song about it."

Joe stands and takes Louise's hand. They dance.

Rick starts his song.

"Hidden hideaway little bird, so happy that I found you. Stay with me forever. Never leave me again."

Rick plays more guitar and Joe takes Chrissie's hand. She follows on to the dance floor and all three dance together with Joe in the middle."

After a while Rick stops playing guitar.

"Chrissie why don't you bring your presents," asks Rick.

Chrissie gazes at him.

"I've seen your beautiful wrapped presents! In your bags! You wanted to surprise us, didn't you?" continues Rick.

Chrissie holds her hand against her forehead.

"Yes. Oh yes. How could I forget?"

In the spare bedroom, Chrissie rumbles through the presents nervously. She takes out a packet and puts that in the bag with the broken boots. She arranges more of the nicely wrapped presents and tries to decide which of the presents she'll give away.

Chrissie enters the living room again with three presents. She turns pale because everybody is away and it's almost dark except one small candlelight. She notices everybody stands in the courtyard. Rick opens the courtyard door ajar.

"Please hide our presents. We won't peek."

He closes the door again. Chrissie hides a red present under the couch cushions. One in a cupboard and one behind the cooker. Rick opens the door ajar without looking inside.

"Can we come in? Are you ready?"

"Done."

They all come inside and giggle when they search for the presents in the dark. Rick is mistaken and touches Chrissie breasts in his search for presents in the half dark room. She withdraws and sinks down on the floor in an empty corner. The dog sits next her and licks her face.

"Sorry about that. I already was thinking it didn't feel like a present. Wrong material," explains Rick.

Joe laughs.

"Haha naughty boy."

"Honestly I didn't see Chrissie. Won't happen again."

"Rick look here instead," says Louise.

Rick finds the red package under the cushion. He looks at Chrissie.

"Is that mine?"

"Yes, it's for you. Do open it."

Joe and Louise find presents and Joe lights a few more candles.

"Almost too beautiful to open," says Rick.

Rick unwraps the gift and finds an expensive man scarf.

"Wow!"

He puts on the scarf and walks around a bit.

"I feel like a proper gentleman."

Louise and Joe unwraps the presents. Louise finds a posh cardigan and Joe finds leather gloves.

Moonlight lights up the courtyard. Chrissie comes in. She closes the door of the house. She wears pyjamas, a pullover and her boots. She walks towards the gates and goes with her hands over it. She finds a small slit to view through. She peers. It's too dark. She inspects the locks. They don't release to open. She stands with her back towards the gates and looks around. She looks at the stars. She whispers.

"Oh my God where am I?"

She turns around and feels the wall to detect cracks. She can't find any. When she passes by the stable, the horse neighs. She halts and waits. The horse is quiet. She continues. She arrives at the side-building. She looks inside via the small windows with curtains. She sees a workbench and carpentry tools. She takes the door latch, opens the door and goes inside.

Chrissie walks around the workroom. She picks up some of the carpentry tools. She sits a short moment in a wooden garden chair with a cushion. She observes piles of new made, small pieces of furniture and carvings on the window ledge, some of these are skeletons of animals in wood. She stands and goes to the window sill. She takes up a ballerina figure carved in wood and admires the beautiful carving. She puts it back.

CHAPTER THREE

It's a sunny winter day. Chrissie sits warmly dressed on a crate. Rick, wearing the new posh scarf, comes out the workroom and brings the garden chair.

"Better take that one."

Chrissie sits on the chair.

"Thank you. You all made that furniture?"

He goes back to the workroom and looks over his shoulder behind.

"Do you want to have a look?"

Chrissie stands and follows him inside.

Chrissie stands in the doorway and Rick planes a piece of wood.

"Do have a look at my carvings."

Chrissie goes to the window sill and takes up the wooden ballerina. Rick continues.

"That's my favourite one. Can you dance?"

"I'm not a ballerina, but yes I can dance."

"I'll take you to a ball!"

Chrissie laughs spontaneously for the first time.

"Cool. But why these skeletons of animal?"

"It's father's hobby. He observes everything in nature, including wildlife."

"Sounds like a biologist."

"Biologist? No biologist. He worked for a mortician when he was young."

He points at a few coffins lids leaning against the wall.

"Sometimes there's a call for one in the nearby villages. Mostly we just trade in furniture."

He nods towards the furniture.

"We'll sell all these. We'll go to a market in two days."

"Where's the market?"

"It's an hour on horse and carriage."

"An hour? Can I come? At least I could make a phone call."

It's full moon. Joe arrives with carriage and horse at the cabin where he found Chrissie. He wears the new leather gloves. The leather gleams in the moonlight. He stops the horse.

"Stop! Stop!"

The horse neighs and stops with a shock. Joe nearly falls off the carriage. Joe steps down. He fastens the horse at a tree. Once this done he stamps the legs of the horse.

"Stupid animal!"

He drinks half a bottle of wine till empty. He flings the bottle on the carriage and takes off the saw and spade.

It's half dark in the hovel. Joe comes in. The moonlight lights up the hovel. He leaves the door open. Half hidden under straw lies the large translucent plastic bag with Katie's body. He takes the saw and inspects it. He walks around a few times inside the hovel. Suddenly he removes the straw with Katie's body inside. He takes up the saw and makes movements like a cross, top to bottom of the bag and then into the other direction. His face has a strange grimace. He howls and places the saw on the plastic bag. He saws the plastic bag in the middle. Sweat drops from his face. Blood spoils the straw. He walks towards the door and observes the moon in a lunar trance. He goes back inside and picks up the saw again. The first part is a hard job because it's Katie's head. His sweat drops on the bag and mingles with the blood. He saws the lowermost part of the torso. He takes a spade and starts digging.

Outside in the fields again, Joe encourages the horse to run fast with a whip.

It doesn't go fast enough for Joe. He stands and hits the horse again.

"Ju! Ju!"

The horse neighs and gallops.

That night Chrissie sits on the bed in the spare room. She sits quietly and then suddenly she browses her bags searching for something nervously. She

21

can't find her mobile. She lies on the bed, staring at the ceiling.

It is a sunny winter day. Only Rick is in the living room and he sits on the couch and plays with Chrissie's mobile. It bleeps at a certain moment. Suddenly Chrissie stands in the doorway and watches Rick's game. She turns pale and quickly grabs her mobile.

"That's mine."

Rick looks surprised.

"What's that Chrissie?"

"You don't know what it is?"

"Sorry, no."

"Do you guys ever go outside this cage?"

Chrissie walks around and tinkers at her mobile. Rick grabs a book from a small table. He stands and goes to the wall with the book-case. His hand goes over the books.

"I'm happy with my books and music. It's peaceful here."

"I just want to go home," says Chrissie.

"You must miss your family. I can understand."

"You know what. It makes sense what you're saying," says Chrissie.

Chrissie sits down on the couch opposite Rick and looks at him.

"Help me to get home!"

Chrissie sits on a crate in the courtyard, dressed with her jacket, hat and scarf. It's a sunny winter day. She watches the activity in the courtyard. Joe and Rick load several pieces of small furniture on the carriage. The dog runs around. The dog hinders Rick.

"Go away, go to Chrissie."

The dog runs around a few more times and then sits down next to Chrissie. Chrissie watches every movement. The dog runs inside the workroom. He barks. He comes back with a piece of bloodied cloth. The cloth fall on the floor. Chrissie picks up the cloth. She notices the blood and throws it away. The dog brings it back to her. She strokes the dog. When loaded, Joe attaches the horse to the carriage. Chrissie stands and walks to the horse.

"I really would like to go to the village."

"It's too cold. We'll call your mother and say you'll be home soon," says Joe.

Joe opens the gates and Rick climbs on the carriage and takes the horse reins. The carriage leaves.

Very quick she runs outside before Joe closes the gate. There're only fields around the house.

"Hey, Chrissie come back!"

Joe runs after her.

"Chrissie come back. You'll get lost."

Joe grabs Chrissie gently. He guides her inside the courtyard.

Rick explains.

"Come on Chrissie. Why do you behave like that now? You must listen to father, he knows what's best for you."

It's dusk. In the courtyard, Chrissie sits on the crate dressed with jacket, hat and scarf. Louise walks from the workroom to the house. She wears the posh cardigan over her other simple cloths. Chrissie looks up when she hears the sound of a horse and carriage arriving. She waits until Louise is in the house. Chrissie heads for the gates and waits silently. There is noise of locks and the gates open outwards. Chrissie runs outside. Rick sits on the carriage. Joe stands with keys in his hands and prevents Chrissie gently from running outside.

"Haha, got you!"

"Did you make a phone call to my parents? What did they say?"

"So sorry. The connection was broke down to the cold temperature."

Joe walks around in the local village shop. He has sugar and fruit in his basket.

When the shopkeeper doesn't watch, he steals a box with sleeping powder sachets and puts it in his pocket. He heads for the till.

"How's Rick?" asks the shopkeeper.

"Great. He's still obsessed with music. I need some more water cans."

"You can take them from the side entrance as usual. How many do you need?"

"Fifty."

The shopkeeper types the amount. Joe browses and he takes up a jigsaw with title "LIFE IN THE COUNTRY" and puts it on the counter.

"Ha, an interesting jigsaw."

Joe puts the jigsaw on the counter.

"That's 28.60 altogether. Where exactly do you live? Nobody seems to know."

Joe pays the requested amount.

"It's rather out-of-the-way. We don't like all that fuss with neighbours and so on. We prefer peace and quiet."

It's a dark and cold night outside in the courtyard. Chrissie wears het jacket over her pyjamas but she shivers. Only the horse can see her. She takes two crates and piles the crates against the gate. She takes a rope and climbs the crates. She wants to attach the rope at the upper end of the gates. She tries things out. She hasn't got enough crates to reach the highest point of the gate to secure the rope.

"Damn not enough crates."

She unties the rope and clambers down. She walks around silently and stands still when the horse neighs. She walks towards the horse and caresses it. She talks to the horse.

"There must be a way out. What do you think?"

She puts the crates back.

The sun shines Chrissie sits at the table with several music magazines. She cuts out a large photo of a musician playing the guitar. A collage lies on the living room floor. She gives the photo to Rick who sits on his knees. He bends over the collage.

"No, not there Rick."

"Why not?"

"The colours doesn't match."

Chrissie grabs the photo, kneels and pastes it somewhere else.

It's almost midnight. Rick and Chrissie paste glue on the back of the collage. They hold the collage against the living room wall to make sure it stays on. Chrissie stands back and looks at the result.

"Wonderful!"

They stand side by side and admire the collage.

In the courtyard the next day, early morning and dawn, Joe pokes a fire with an iron stick. On the ground lies cloths of a woman. He throws wood on the fire. The fire gets bigger. Joe has a satisfied expression on his face. He takes some old rags with blood stains. He throws it on the fire and pokes again. After this has disappeared in the flames, he takes a pair of woman's shoes. Smoke gets bigger from the burning of the leather shoes. He coughs and waves the smoke away. He heads for the house.

In the living room Joe goes to the stove and prepares his coffee. He drinks a mouthful. Accidental he looks around and notices the collage. He's baffled.

"What's that rubbish at the wall?"

He puts down his cup. He tears the collage off the wall.

"Bloody hell!"

Back in the courtyard, Joe flings the collage on the fire. He pokes the remaining parts of the burning shoes and waves away the smoke produced by the burning shoes.

Rick comes in the living room. He yawns and he rubs his eyes.

"Aah."

The door is ajar and smokes comes in. Rick closes the door. He goes to the stove and takes coffee. He sits down at the table and drinks. He looks at the wall and doesn't notice the collage. He drinks another mouthful and looks around. He can't find the collage. He stands and looks through the window and sees pieces of the burning collage on the fire. Rick runs outside. He tries to save the part of the burning collage still intact. His father gives him a hit on the arm with the iron stick. Rick bleeds.

"Get back, get back you!"

Chrissie stands in the doorway and watches with open mouth. Rick pulls back. Joe points the stick threateningly at Rick and Chrissie.

"Both of you know nothing about life."

It's day and Joe enters the room carrying the jigsaw from the shop "LIFE IN THE COUNTRY".

Rick just told his mother what happened.

"You shouldn't have done that Joe," says Louise.

"I know darling."

Joe kisses Louise and goes to Rick and Chrissie who eat breakfast at the table.

"Sorry kid I really lost my temper."

Joe lays the jigsaw on the table.

"I hope that this can make it up again."

Rick watches the jigsaw. After a while he opens the box and takes out the pieces. Louise sits down also and admires the jigsaw. Louise and Rick start sorting out the jigsaw.

Late evening in the living room Chrissie winds a bandage around Rick's arm.

"This bandage will be better. Your dad lost his mind! It's frightening."

"Thanks Chrissie. I don't understand why dad behaved like that. He'll help you getting to London."

"I'm so happy about that. We can meet in London."

"I couldn't survive in the city. Why don't you come back in summer? Promise me! I'll miss you so much."

"Well maybe I go camping next vacation with some friends. Join us!"

"I would like to. What a great idea! I've never been on a camping holiday."

Rick kisses Chrissie's hand. He holds her hand. Chrissie smiles. Rick takes the guitar and plays songs for Chrissie. She listens quietly. Rick points at the window.

"Look at the moon. Let's have a walk outside."

The moon lights the courtyard. Rick and Chrissie, wearing coats, walk hand in hand. Rick hums a song and they dance. Rick kisses her. He takes her hand and heads for the workroom.

"Let's go inside. I'll put on the gas burner."

They sit both on the armchair in the workroom. A small gas burner heats the room.

He kisses Chrissie passionate. He takes off her sweater and admires her. He kisses her breasts.

"You're beautiful"

She takes off his sweater. He caresses her hair and kisses her. He pulls her on the ground. He takes the cushion from the garden chair and throws it on the ground. He pulls her on the cushion and they make love. Behind Chrissie the moon shines on the coffin lids, leaning against the wall.

CHAPTER FOUR

A few days later Joe and Louise are in the living room. Joe eats soup and a piece of bread. He dips the bread in the soup. A large pan of soup stands on the stove. Louise stirs the soup. She goes outside. Joe immediately stands when Louise has left the room. He takes a sachet of sleeping powder out his pocket. He tears the sachet and pours the powder in the soup. He puts the empty sachet in the bin. He stirs the soup. He goes back to the table when he sees that his wife arrives. He continues eating his soup.

"I love that soup!"

Louise laughs. Joe grabs her when she passes by and he pulls her on his knees. They kiss and he caresses her. Louise withdraws.

"Stop it. Not at this time."

She stands and arranges her clothes. She takes a plate of potatoes and sits opposite Joe. She starts peeling the potatoes while Joe eats his soup.

"You make my heart thump louder darling!"

"Sometimes I worry about Rick. He could have his own family by now."

"He's still young."

"He suffered when Katie left. It was such a good friend for him."

Joe finishes his soup and stands. He caresses his wife when he walks behind her.

"No worries, darling."

Late evening Chrissie and Rick sit side by side on the couch. Joe leaves the living room, looking back at Louise.

"Louise, bedtime now?"

Louise follows.

"Good night mum."

Rick takes his guitar and plays a song.

"One day a beautiful girl arrived. She makes my heart thump louder."

Chrissie sits back and dreams away while he plays guitar.

"That's very beautiful."

"I wrote that song for you."

"I hope your father takes me to the village, as promised."

"I'll miss you so much."

"I'm looking forward that we can hook up again in the spring. I must return to work and my parents 'll be sick with worry at my absence!"

He takes her hand and they sit quiet for a moment. Chrissie sits back and closes her eyes. Rick sits back also and yawns. He rubs his eyes.

"Damn I feel so tired."

He puts the guitar away and takes Chrissie in his arms. They both close their eyes. Joe comes inside. He has a nasty grimace on his face when he sees Rick and Chrissie sleeping.

The next day Chrissie sits on a crate in the courtyard next to the window. Louise and Rick are in the workroom. Joe heads for the house. Accidental she peers through the window of the house. She notices Joe pouring something in the soup. She follows his moves. When the sachet is empty, Joe crumples the sachet and puts it in the bin.

That same night Chrissie slips into the living room wearing her pyjamas. The moon lights the room. She heads for the bin and browses. She takes out the sachet and rubs it. She reads the label. It reads sleeping powder. She turns pale.

"Bastard!"

She puts the sachet in her pocket.

At midday they all have dinner. Chrissie refuses the soup Louise ladles out for her.

"Thank you Louise. I don't feel very well today."

Joe stands at the till and looks at her.

"Are you not hungry Chrissie?"

"I hope you can bring me to the village as agreed."

"I'll. I've to finish that job first."

Louise and Joe left the room. Chrissie and Rick sit together on the couch. Chrissie takes the empty sachet out her pocket and shows it to Rick.

"Look at the label!"

"What do you mean?"

"That's what your father pours in our soup."

Rick takes the sachet and reads the label.

"That's why," Chrissie explains.

"Why what?"

Chrissie stands and walks around.

"Don't you realize Rick? We always fall asleep because your father pours sleeping powder in the soup."

Rick watches her silently. Then he stands and walks around with the label.

"Why shouldn't I ask him."

Chrissie pulls his arm.

"No. Be careful. I don't trust your dad."

"No worries Chrissie."

Rick tears away and disappears.

Rick enters the workroom. Joe doesn't look up. Rick throws the empty sachet on the workbench.

"What's that?"

Joe casts a glance at the sachet and continues his work. He looks over his shoulder at Rick and snorts.

"What?"

Rick points at the sachet.

"Why're you pouring that stuff in our soup?"

"Haha, what're you talking about? I don't understand. Is Chrissie telling you that? It's for your mother's health. Have you forgotten she has a heart condition?"

Rick enters the living room again. Chrissie sits on the couch.

"What did he say?"

Rick sits down and kisses her.

"Chrissie, you don't understand, it's for mother's heart condition!"

"We don't have a heart condition do we?"

"You're joking. I lost my heart for you."

"I'm not joking. I'm frightened. Your father promised to take me to the village but he didn't."

He tries to kiss her but she withdraws. He gives up.

"I've some work to do," says Rick.

Rick leaves and Chrissie jumps up and heads for the bin. She opens the bin and vomits. And again.

Rick notices from outside she's not well and enters again. He touches shoulder.

"Are you ill?"

He hastily takes a cloth and cleans her face. He leads her to the table.

"Do sit down Chrissie, relax!"

He opens a bottle and pours water in a cup for Chrissie. He watches while she drinks it slowly.

He caresses her shoulders.

"Do you feel better?"

Chrissie nods.

"We must get away from here. We've to find a way."

Rick caresses her hair.

"I can't leave my family. So I'll wait till you come back."

It's late evening and Rick lays his book on the floor and takes Chrissie's hand.

"You're so quiet? I'm tired."

"You're still looking pale.

Chrissie looks away.

"I go to bed early."

Chrissie stands. She kisses Rick good night. He pulls her on his lap. They sit quiet for a moment in each other's arms. He caresses her. She withdraws and leaves the room.

Chrissie enters the spare bedroom. Tears roll silently from her face when she falls on the bed. She lies awake and listens to the sounds of the house. Suddenly she stands and dresses with as many clothes as possible. Finally she puts on her scarf, hat and gloves. She puts her mobile in her pocket and a bottle of beer inside her coat. She slips outside.

CHAPTER FIVE

In the courtyard the moon shines. Chrissie piles the crates. The crates reach the upper end of the gates. She makes a staircase with three other crates and climbs the piled crates. She attaches the rope at the upper end and lets the rope hang at the other side. She climbs over the gate. Chrissie hangs at the rope. She holds the rope tight with her gloves and sinks down. She lands with a plop. The horse in the courtyard neighs. Immediately she runs away and doesn't stop.

It's dawn. Chrissie enters the streets of a very small village. Everybody is still asleep. A van stands at the village shop. A man wants to enter his van. Chrissie runs towards him.

"Hello."

"Yes?"

"Where are you going?"

"I'm going straight off to London."

"Please can you give me a lift?"

"Okay. Jump in."

She heads for the passenger side of the van and opens the door.

It's day and Chrissie is asleep as the van enters London's suburbs. The man shakes Chrissie's arm.

"Darling. Wakey, wakey."

Chrissie wakes with a shock. She looks around bewildered.

"Almost reached my destination. Where shall I drop you?"

Chrissie walks towards the door of her own house. She rings the bell. Her mother opens the door.

"Oooh Chrissie."

They embrace.

"What happened? You've been away several days! The police was looking for you."

"I'm alright mum."

One hour later Chrissie sits with pyjamas and wet hair at the kitchen table. From time to time she eats a bit of breakfast. Doreen sits opposite her with a cup of tea. She sits before a laptop answering an email and talking via the mobile to the office.

"Look, I try to give a quick response now to all these emails that came in. I pop in the office late afternoon. Have to sleep a few hours first. Bye."

"The police could arrive in a few minutes. Finish your breakfast first," says Doreen.

"I'll finish first that email."

"Sure darling. Let's contact the GP to check you over."

"Not necessary mum."

Mother's mobile rings. She answers.

"Yes Gary she's back. She's having breakfast. I still can't believe!"

She puts her mobile down.

"Your father has been worried sick about you."

Doreen takes an empty can from the table and stands. She hesitates and sits down again.

"You have to tell the police what happened! That nasty Santa. The guy is an abductor," says Doreen.

"I'll tell them everything what I know. I hope the problems with my stolen credit card can be solved soon."

"It's very strange that family. They confused sleeping powder with medication for heart condition," continues Doreen.

"It is indeed. I've only seen once. But I was freezing and they rescued me in that hovel! They were very kind. The father could lose his temper from time to time but he always apologized," explains Chrissie.

"And that you had totally no freedom at all to leave that house?" asks Doreen.

"It was a very remote location. I even can't remember the name of that village. I walked the most of the night after climbing over the wall and was desperate to get home," says Chrissie.

"They should be able to track that abductor Santa," says Doreen.

Chrissie yawns.

A few days later Chrissie works out on a bike. Loud music sounds. Chrissie reduces speed. On the bike next to her works out red haired girlfriend, Charlene.

"What's up? Are you tired?"

"Nothing is up."

"You're not so chatty anymore. I miss the old Chrissie."

"Yes, well."

"What?"

"I'm in love."

"Who is it? Anyone I know?"

"Well."

"Well what? Someone you met in the country?"

A few weeks later Chrissie, dressed for the office, inspects her mirror in the bathroom.

She takes a pregnancy test and anxiously observes the confirmation of either positive or negative. The test result is "pregnant".

She vomits in the toilet. She washes her face at the sink.

It's almost spring when Chrissie and Charlene sit side by side on Charlene's bed. It's dark outside. They share a tablet and browse the web for camping sites

Charlene chooses a site.

"Look at that one."

"Brilliant. Look Charlene, I hope you don't mind if I leave you behind at the campsite."

"No problem."

They browse google maps.

"I'm pleased that you have offered to help. I'm really desperate. I have to talk with Rick. If it wasn't for you, mum would never allow me to go."

Charlene browses fast. On screen the train station of a small village pops up.

"Bingo, that's the nearest train station! We can take our bikes on the train," says Charlene.

CHAPTER SIX

It's a nice early spring day. Chrissie loads the last bag with camping gear on her bike. Her mother Doreen stands at the front door and watches. Charlene waits already on her bike.

Once Chrissie's rucksack is in position she kisses her mum goodbye.

"Take care!"

Chrissie heads for her bike.

"Bye Charlene, keep an eye on Chrissie," says Doreen.

"Trust me!"

They leave.

The next morning Charlene stands in front of her tent on the camping site. Chrissie attaches her bag on the bike. She wears shorts and a top. Chrissie wants to travel solo.

"I'll leave you now. Enjoy the holiday," says Chrissie.

They kiss each other goodbye.

"Take care! Do send me a text from time to time."

Chrissie goes back to her bike.

"If there is mobile connectivity. Not quite sure there is."

"Do send me a picture of your mystery lover!"

Chrissie cycles away and looks back over her shoulder.

They wave goodbye.

"Bye sweets."

"Love you!"

Chrissie arrives in a small village on her bike. She stops and takes a map. She studies the map for a couple of seconds a few moments and leaves.

It's dusk. Chrissie cycles through fields. She stops the bike. She heads for a tree and loads off her luggage. She sets the tent for the night.

Early morning and Chrissie exits the tent and stretches her arms pointing to the sky. A small kettle stands on a very small camping-stove. The smart phone music is on. She exercises to rapid beats of the music. When she finishes the work out, she prepares a cup of coffee. She sits. She drinks the coffee and eats a piece of bread.

Chrissie cycles through fields. She arrives on her bike at the cabin where Joe found her. She stops and parks the bike. She heads for the door of the hovel. She opens the door. It's dark inside the hovel. She walks around and sniffs. She immediately sets the door wide open and waves with her hand.

"What a smell!"

She finds a spade in the corner. She takes the spade up and puts it down again. She leaves.

It's dusk. Chrissie stands in a field. She turns and watches, binoculars attached to her eyes. Bike on the floor. Through the binoculars she spots the railway line she has seen when she was abducted. She puts the binoculars down and surveys the view of the horizon. She returns the binoculars to her bag and takes out a bottle of coke. She drinks. She puts the bottle away. She takes her mobile and notices the signal icon. She immediately opens the picture Charlene sent. A jolly Charlene pops up, next to a nice bloke. Chrissie smiles. She puts her mobile away and climbs on the bike again.

It's dark outside. Chrissie crawls inside the tent. She organizes the airbed to slot in comfortably to the length of the tent, allocating space for her bundle of clothes. In her half zipped rucksack stacked neatly inside are two bottles, two tins of food, bread and biscuits. She stoops as she gets out the tent. Trees and bushes conceal the tent. Chrissie closes off the zip fastening the tent. She shivers. She closes her vest. She heads for Rick's house, a mile away from the tent.

Once she arrives, she steps with slow deliberation around the house of Rick, Joe and Louise. She listens hard to the dormant of the courtyard. No voices enter this space. At the wooden gate she finds a small slit. She peers inside but can't see anything. She sits with her back against the wooden gates. After a while she hears a noise. She stands and listens.

Inside the courtyard Joe heads for the workroom. Joe goes inside the workroom. The light inside the workroom goes on for a short time. The light fades out and Joe steps outside. He goes back to the house. Joe goes inside the house.

Chrissie still sits with her back on the wooden gates relaxed but alert. She hears a cough. At the same time the horse neighs. She reflexively gets up.

"Rick!"

Rick heads for the workroom. He stops immediately and listens.

"Chrissie? Is that you?"

"Quiet Rick, shussh. Come over here."

Rick heads for the gate. He holds his head against the gate.

"Chrissie darling. How come you're here?"

"I've come for you. Don't say anything."

"I don't believe."

"No time to waste. Pile up those crates and just climb."

Rick looks around and sees the ladder. The horse neighs.

"Hold on a sec, I'll grab dad's new ladder."

Rick heads for the horse. He caresses it and whispers.

"Easy. It's Chrissie. Can you believe it?"

The horse is quiet and Rick puts the ladder against the wall. He climbs and can see Chrissie. He climbs on the wall and lifts the ladder to the other side.

Chrissie holds the ladder and Rick descends. He embraces Chrissie. They kiss.

"Let's go to my tent."

She takes his hand. They run towards the tent.

They lie naked side by side on the air bed, still holding each other. Rick withdraws from Chrissie.

"I have to go back. Come with me."

"I can't. I have to tell you something."

"What?"

Rick dresses and wants to leave.

"Wait."

"I have to leave."

"Wait Rick. I…"

Rick opens the tent. He goes outside. Chrissie follows.

Rick embraces Chrissie.

"It's too late now."

"Are you coming back tomorrow?"

Rick caresses Chrissie's hair.

"Definitely. I'll arrive earlier and stay later. Bring you some food."

After a last kiss Rick runs back to the house.

The next evening Rick and Chrissie sit naked opposite each other on the air bed in the dark. Rick covers the blanket over his shoulder and Chrissie's. They play and cuddle each other. Chrissie falls on her belly.

"Ouch. Watch out."

Rick helps her up again.

"Did I hurt you?"

"I've to tell you something very important."

"What?"

"I'm pregnant."

Rick face looks ashen.

"Chrissie?"

"I'm telling you the truth."

Rick embraces Chrissie.

"Chrissie darling."

He kisses her.

"Gonna be a dad! Gawd almighty!"

They lie and caress each other.

It's a sunny day and Chrissie sits before her tent. She surveys the view of the horizon. Joe heads for the house, with his horse and carriage. He disappears in the courtyard. Chrissie takes her bike and leaves in the opposite direction.

Chrissie browses around in the local shop. She buys bread, a tin of soup, cheese and apples. Before going to the till she takes a large can of water.

"You're new in town?"

"No, I'm here for a countryside break."

"By yourself?"

"With a friend actually. It's very pleasant here."

"Take care won't you. Last year a girl went missing. The police conducted a huge search for her."

"Really?"

"Still missing and no clue to her whereabouts!"

Rick and Chrissie sit outside the tent. It's midnight. They eat cold drumsticks and cold potatoes.

"That's what they said in the shop, says Chrissie."

"It's a mystery indeed," replies Rick

"I can't stay long here. Come with me to London."

"Cannot stomach London. No, not that place."

The following night Chrissie stands when Rick arrives. They embrace and kiss each other.

"Finally. You're late."

They sit side by side before the tent.

Rick plays with a leaf.

He sits with his head between his legs, looking down at the ground.

"You're a father now to our baby. You've a duty to both of us to come."

"I'm thinking Chrissie, really. I'm thinking at mum also."

"Think at the child. We love each other!"

Rick stands and walks around. He breaks off another bough from a nearby tree and slashes more pieces. He throws the pieces on the ground. He stands with his back before Chrissie.

"I hope it's a girl."

He sits again and embraces Chrissie.

"I'm so happy. And frightened all the same. Very strange feeling."

"You've to make a decision. You can't stay with your parent your whole life. And also that sleeping powder your father puts in the food."

"That was only once, mother was not well."

He kisses her.

"My Chrissie. Tomorrow night we leave!"

Rick climbs down the ladder. Once he is on the ground in the courtyard, he takes the ladder and puts it at the other end of the courtyard against the wall. Joe stands before the window of his bedroom and watches him.

It's day. In the living room Rick browses his books in the bookcase. He takes out a book. He opens the book and reads. On the floor sits a rucksack. He takes another book out the rucksack. He puts it back in the bookcase. He flings the new book in the rucksack. He browses again. He walks around and takes up his guitar. He puts it next to the rucksack. He arranges the clothes under the books. Again he browses the bookcase. His mother comes in and he hides his rucksack.

CHAPTER SEVEN

Chrissie sleeps on the air bed in the tent. It's dark. Suddenly the zip fastening of the tent opens. Chrissie wakes up. Joe's head appears and Chrissie screams.

"Do come inside Chrissie! Why're you sleeping in that tent? It's far too dangerous."

"Where is Rick?"

"Rick's waiting for you in the house. Follow me. Louise will cook a nice meal for you."

Chrissie stands and zips up the tent. She walks with Joe towards the house.

"I prefer sleeping in the tent anyway. No worries about food. I'll not bother you. I'm not coming inside. I just want to talk to Rick."

"As you wish. Great you came to visit us. You're welcome anytime."

The following night Chrissie waits for Rick again. He doesn't come. She walks towards the house and is surprised to find out that the gates are open. Rick runs at Chrissie who stands in the gate opening and embraces her.

"Dad didn't want me to leave."

Very fast Joe appears and he closes the gates. Chrissie reacts.

"Hey, hey. I want to go back to my tent."

Chrissie tears away from Rick and wants to push the gates open again but they don't give.

"No worry love, everything's alright. You don't have to sleep in that tent again. It makes sense what dad says."

Later that night Chrissie sits on the single bed in the spare bedroom. Rick slips inside. He goes to Chrissie. He sits on the bed. Chrissie walks around the room and talks excitedly but not loud enough to wake up his parents.

"I want to leave as fast as possible. There is no way we're staying here."

"We'll leave. We'll find something. Unfortunately he took away the ladder."

"We need to take away his keys."

"There must be spare keys indeed."

The next morning. Rick enters the bedroom of Joe and Louise. He kneels and knocks softly with his hand on the wooden floorboards. He repeatedly knocks at a certain floorboard because it's a hollow sound. He tries to lift the floorboard. It lifts up easily and he sees an iron box. He tries to open the box but it's closed. He looks over the box.

"Damn it's locked tight."

He shakes the box and can hear the sound of iron objects inside the box.

Chrissie's working out in the living room. She stretches. Rick enters.

"I found the box with the spare keys."

Chrissie stops and kisses Rick.

"That's great news. Can't wait."

"We only have to find another pair of keys to open that box! We've to be careful. Dad 'll be back any moment now."

Chrissie stretches again. Rick imitates her and asks advice

"Like that?"

"Yes!"

They laugh and continue. Chrissie leads.

Later Rick and Chrissie run in circles side by side in the courtyard. The dog follows and barks. They laugh when the dogs hinders Chrissie.

"Go away, says Chrissie."

The dog barks. After a while the dog heads for the gates and barks again. There is the noise of Joe's carriage arriving at the other side.

"He's coming!"

They disappear inside.

Rick and Chrissie laugh when they come inside, still running.

Louise prepares the food.

"Why do you laugh?"

Rick starts playing the guitar. Chrissie goes to Louise. She takes a plate and helps Louise preparing the vegetables.

"I'm so happy that you're back Chrissie. Rick was very sad without you."

"Mum, don't talk like that! Chrissie wants to be free."

"But you both want to be together, right?"

"Right mum, I want to be with Chrissie. Never forget I love you. you're the best mum of the world. It's so difficult!"

"What's difficult?" asks Louise.

Afternoon and Rick cycles around in the courtyard on Chrissie's bike. Chrissie sits on a crate. Rick stops before her.

"Hop on the back of the bike!"

"No. It's useless we can't go anywhere."

"Let's just have some fun."

He reaches his hand. Chrissie takes his hand and he pulls her. She stands and he almost falls with the bike. They laugh. She hops on the back of the bike and they cycle in circles.

"Stop, I'm getting dizzy."

Rick stops and she jumps off the bike. She goes back to the crate. Rick cycles more.

"I can't cycle enough."

The next day Chrissie stands before the door of her bedroom. The door is ajar. She watches Joe who enters his bedroom. Joe walks inside his bedroom. He hasn't noticed Chrissie. He goes to the back of the door. He leaves the door half open. He makes a noise with an object. He heads for the floorboard with a small object in his hand. It's the same floorboard that Rick has inspected. He kneels and looks behind him. He stands up again and shuts the door first.

Chrissie stands in the bedroom of Joe and Louise behind the door. The door is ajar. She searches with her hand the backside of the door and then the wall next to the door. She finds a hidden crack. She feels inside with her hand and finds a small key. She puts it back and slips outside.

In the evening Rick slips inside the bedroom of Joe and Louise and searches for the crack in the wall behind the door. Chrissie stands at the door and points at the hidden crack.

"There!"

He finds the small key. He heads for the floorboard. He takes out the iron box and opens the box with the small key. He finds the large keys and takes these out. He closes the iron box again.

"Hurry up!"

Next evening Chrissie and Rick sit quiet on the couch. The dog is asleep. They both read magazines.

Louise arranges a few pots in the kitchen corner and leaves for the bedroom. They watch Louise's moves.

"Good night, says Louise."

Rick stands and kisses his mother. He embraces her.

"Night mum, love you so much."

Rick goes back to his seat and hides behind a music magazine. Once Louise has left the room, they both jump up. Rick embraces and fondles the dog.

"I'll miss you."

The dog makes whimpering noises and lies down again.

Once in the courtyard Rick and Chrissie attach luggage to the bike, in a somewhat hidden corner of the courtyard. They are both wearing rucksacks. Rick opens the gates a bit, just enough to slip outside. Chrissie walks outside with the bike. Rick follows Chrissie outside.

CHAPTER EIGHT

It's dawn. Rick and Chrissie cycle through the field. Rick steers and Chrissie sits behind him. They notice the hovel.

"That's the cabin where your father found me."

"Never been here."

"I found utensils inside, maybe your father's."

"Let's have a stop here."

Chrissie and Rick browse around in the hovel. Rick uses the spade to separate the straw. Some fresh earth appears. Rick goes over it with the spade. "There must have been a hole here."

He examines a bit longer.

"Something must be buried here."

He starts to dig. The longer he digs, the smell gets stronger. Chrissie sniffs and turns away.

"It's that strange smell again."

"Must be a dead animal."

Rick digs deeper. Chrissie draws back.

"I'll wait for you outside."

Chrissie and Rick sit against the wooden wall of the hovel.

"Let's go. Why bury an animal inside a hovel?"

"There's something not right in there."

Rick stands and wants to enter the hovel again.

"Don't go inside again!"

"Just a sec."

He goes inside. After a while he comes out again with glasses surrounded by mud. Chrissie stands and draws back.

"What's that in your hands?"

49

Rick looks devastated and sits down again. He places the glasses on the ground.

"They're Katie's glasses."

"Katie's glasses?"

"She probably lost her glasses here."

Chrissie goes back to the bike.

"Let's go."

Rick doesn't react.

"Rick now! Let's go."

Rick straddles the bike. Chrissie sits behind. Rick cycles fast.

Later that day Chrissie and Rick notice a few trees.

"Let's stop!"

Rick stops. Chrissie jumps off the bike. She shakes her legs and arms. Rick heads for the trees. He parks the bike against a tree. They take off their rucksacks. They sit down side by side. He takes out a bottle of beer and two plastic cups. He takes out bread, cheese and a small knife. He pours the beer in the cups.

"Are you hungry?"

Chrissie nods. Rick cuts the bread and the cheese with the knife. He gives Chrissie a piece of bread and cheese.

"Strange these glasses. You didn't tell me anything about Katie. Was she your girlfriend? You told me you had a few girlfriends before me."

"Let's not talk about that. Let's think about our future now. I'll be a father in five months."

Chrissie takes the bread. They drink the beer and eat. Chrissie sighs.

"Let's go to London. Far enough from everything here."

"I can't do it. I couldn't survive with all these strange people around me. No way!"

"I've to contact my parents. Otherwise they'll consider me dead."

"I would lose you and the child when you do that. I already explained. I can't agree with that."

"How're we going to cope here?"

"No worries. I'm a handy man."

"With a baby?"

"We'll find something. We make a cosy home for the baby. I have saved money. We can buy things."

"You must understand that I've left my whole life behind me."

"Likewise. You don't understand. I just lost my family because you wanted to leave. We've to think at the child. At first it needs a mum and a dad."

It's dusk. They cycle not far from railway tracks. Rick steers. Chrissie's behind him. In the distance they see a dark object. Chrissie points at it.

"What's that?"

"Something big for sure."

After a while they arrive at an old railway carriage. They park the bike, take off their rucksacks and head for the door. Rick pulls the door. They both go inside. They look around. It's a rather clean old carriage. Rick sits on one of the seats and pulls Chrissie on his lap.

"What do you think?"

Chrissie looks around.

"Mmm I don't know."

"Here we're safe. Nobody will find us here."

Rick stands and goes outside. Chrissie walks and inspects the carriage. Rick comes back with the bags. He takes out all the food and puts it on a table. Rick takes out the blankets. He lies down on a seat and tries to find the best position.

"I prefer this instead of the tent. Don't you?"

It's a sunny day and Rick's busy outside with the kettle. He takes two cups of coffee and goes inside the railway carriage. Chrissie still sleeps, lying on a carriage seat. He caresses her hair and she awakes. She looks around.

"I didn't realize at first where I was."

Rick hands over the coffee. They sit side by side and drink coffee.

"Thanks Rick."

Rick stands and goes around the carriage.

"Here's where the kitchen will go."

He goes to the other side.

"That's the best view. That's our sitting-room."

He goes to the darkest corner.

"That's for sleeping. We can build a wall here."

He shows where the wall could be build. Chrissie turns pale.

"We can't survive here."

Chrissie suddenly runs outside.

Chrissie runs to a tree. She bends over and vomits. Rick follows.

"It's the baby. He or she agrees with me. I hope it's a girl."

Rick goes inside. Rick is back with toilet paper and a cup with water. He cleans Chrissie's face with the toilet paper. He hands over the cup for Chrissie to drink from.

The next day Rick and Chrissie stand before a highway. Opposite is a mall. Rick holds the bike. At the other side of the highway is a shopping mall. Rick is mesmerized by the cars. He follows with his eyes one car after another. His head turns several times.

"That many cars!"

"Let's park the bike here and cross the road."

Rick parks the bike but still watches the cars.

"Wow!"

He points at a sleek car.

"I would like to sit in one of these."

Chrissie looks at the distant sky. They wait for the appropriate moment.

"After that one. Let's go!"

They climb over a low fence and cross the highway.

Chrissie and Rick come out the shopping mall and head for the highway. They both carry a new rucksack and several bags. Rick carries along his side a brand new bike. When they arrive at the highway, Rick parks his bike and watches the cars.

"All that noise!"

He looks over his new bike. Rick tinkers at the bike.

"It's a great bike."

"Let's cross the road first."

When it's quiet Rick picks up the bike as they clamber over the fence. Rick almost falls due to extra burden of bike and bags.

"Watch out!"

They cross the road.

CHAPTER NINE

It's a sunny day. Rick carves a cradle from a chunk of tree. Chrissie sits on a foldable chair next to the carriage and reads a book. Chrissie's belly shows she's pregnant. Rick stops his work and looks with satisfaction at the cradle.

"Almost finished. What do you think?"

Chrissie stands and looks at the cradle.

"Wonderful."

She embraces Rick and they kiss.

"We're so lucky!"

It's night and Joe walks around the carriage. He notices the cradle placed outside. He shakes his head in disbelief. He peers through the window and sees Rick playing the guitar and the pregnant Chrissie sitting cosy at a table, while reading.

"Well a baby on its way!" says Joe.

He walks around a few times. He leaves.

The following evening Chrissie sits on a couch reading a magazine. The cradle's docked in the corner with blankets and smooth bear. The room is illuminated by candles. Rick reads a book. Suddenly they hear the noise of a car arriving. The lamps of the car lights up the room. Rick heads for the door. The car trumpets. Rick opens the door. Ellen, a forty year old nurse stands in the doorway.

"Do come in!"

Ellen enters.

"Hi, how're you?"

She kisses Chrissie on the cheek.

"Thanks for coming."

Ellen puts the suitcase on the table and opens it. She takes out a manometer.

"Now let's have a look at mother and baby."

Twenty minutes later Rick and Ellen head for the car. Ellen steps inside. Rick holds open the car door and leans on it with his arm.

"I don't know what we could've done without you Ellen."

"Again, I urge you to get in contact with social services. Social housing is an option to consider."

"First the baby. Let's hope it all goes okay."

Rick whips nervously on both his legs. Ellen is keen to shut the door, but Rick prevents her.

"Everything will be all right. Don't worry. Chrissie's very healthy."

"I hope it'll."

"I explained everything!"

"Thanks a lot!"

He shuts the door and the car leaves.

Rick goes inside and lays his ear on Chrissie's tummy.

"I can hear the baby."

He stands and walks around the room. He goes back to Chrissie and kneels. He caresses her tummy.

"I really hope it's a girl."

He lays his head on her tummy.

"A girl just like you."

"We'll wait and see."

The cat rubs Chrissie's legs. Rick picks up the cat and proceeds talking to the cat.

"What do you think?"

Four weeks later the nurse gently scoops up the freshly cleaned new-born and lays the naked baby on Chrissie's tummy.

Rick runs around like crazy with towels. On the floor there 're buckets of water strewn around, some contain dirty towels. On the table is the baby-bath.

"Congrats. Have you decided about the girl's name?" asks Ellen.

Rick caresses the baby with a beaming smile.

"It's Phoebe!"

Ellen gathers her instruments and gets ready for leaving.

"Well, Phoebe's very healthy."

It's still day and Chrissie sits on the couch. She breast feeds the baby. Rick sits opposite to Chrissie. He watches with a happy smile on his face. He caresses the child with a smile on his face.

"My little girl!"

CHAPTER TEN

The cradle with Phoebe stands next to the carriage. The sun shines. Chrissie rocks the cradle. She holds a tinkling toy above the cradle and produces sounds with it. She tries to get the attention of the baby.

"Hey Phoebe, hey, hey."

At the back of the carriage Joe hides. He carries a bag. He waits until Chrissie goes inside. Once Chrissie disappears inside the carriage, he goes to the baby who is silent. He picks up Phoebe and gently sways it in his arms.

"Say hi to your grandad!"

He opens the bag and he puts the baby inside, together with one blanket. He ignores the cat. He runs towards the trees, absorbing himself amid the woods.

Inside the carriage Chrissie arranges the kitchen tools. She produces a lot a noise. The cat enters and meows. Chrissie strokes the cat.

"Time for some milk."

She pours some milk into the cat bowl. The cat drinks the milk. She washes a few more pans. The cat has drunk all the milk and comes to Chrissie again. Chrissie strokes the cat.

"What's wrong with you?"

The cat goes outside and Chrissie follows. Chrissie notices suddenly the empty cradle.

"No! Phoebe!"

Chrissie in aghast horror and disbelief turns over the blanket in the cradle.

"Phoebe, Phoebe, Rick, Rick!"

She looks around as far as she can. She runs around the carriage and ends up again at the empty cradle. She runs fast for the trees. She finds nothing there. After a while she takes the bike and cycles around looking for the baby.

Rick arrives on his bike and finds an empty cradle. He goes to the doorway of the carriage and sees that nobody is inside. He walks around the carriage.

"Chrissie!"

He almost steps on the cat. Chrissie just arrives with the bike. She looks bewildered. He lays his hands on her face.

"Chrissie, Chrissie. What happened?"

"The baby, the baby! Gone! She was in the cradle. I was washing up inside."

Rick inspects the cradle.

"Damn! Maybe it's father who found us. I heard some noise last week. For a second I imagined him walking around. I just forgot about it."

"You forgot? Why didn't you tell me?"

A few hours later Joe arrives with the horse-drawn carriage in the courtyard. He shuts the gates. He looks around and doesn't notice his wife. He heads for the house. He opens the door.

"Louise!"

He goes back to the horse. His wife follows. He takes out the baby and laughs.

"Here it is. Our grandchild! It's a girl!"

The baby starts to cry. Louise takes the baby and cuddles it.

"Oooh is that our beautiful granddaughter? What a surprise!"

"That ruttish son of yours wanted to abduct our grandchild!"

Louise goes inside with the baby and cuddles it.

"I'm so happy!"

Back at the railway carriage Chrissie and Rick stand outside at the empty cradle.

Chrissie shouts at Rick.

"It's your fault. You said we're safe here!"

"He never would've found us in London!"

It's a cloudy evening. Chrissie and Rick cycle in the direction of the house of Joe and Louise. They head for the trees. They conceal their bike underneath bushes. They run towards the house. They walk around the house. The dog sniffs and barks when they pass by the gates. Rick takes Chrissie's hand and they run at the other side. Rick whispers.

"Let's wait here, he can't smell us here."

They listen and hear the noise of the carriage being attached at the horse. Rick whispers.

"He'll come out."

They hear the noise of rattling keys. Rick and Chrissie shove silent to the gate. The moment the gate opens outwards, they hide just behind the gate. Rick holds his arm before Chrissie's waist. He whispers.

"We sneak inside as the carriage comes out."

"How'll we get out again?"

"We leave again before he comes back."

The carriage with Joe comes out. Rick takes Chrissie's hand and they run very fast inside. Joe doesn't notice.

They hide in a corner of the courtyard. They sit down. The dog runs at Rick. He's able to silence the dog. Joe closes the gates from the other side. Keys rattle. They hear the noise of horse and carriage leaving. When this noise disappears Chrissie rises. Rick stops her.

"Wait a moment."

He stands instead.

"I'll go in alone. Wait here."

Chrissie wants to rise again.

"No Rick I want to see Phoebe."

Rick pushes her back to sit on the ground.

"Please wait here. First I have to talk to mother alone."

Chrissie sinks down again. The dog sniffs at her. She embraces the dog.

Rick heads for the house. He peers through the window before opening the door.

In the living room, the baby sleeps in one of the couches. Louise looks up when she hears the noise of the door opening. She lets a cup drop. Rick runs towards his mum and they embrace each other. While embracing her he looks over her shoulder. With relief he notices the baby. He closes his eyes for a brief moment.

"I'm back mother!"

"I'm so proud of the baby."

He lets Louise loose. He picks up Phoebe and goes to the door, baby in his arms. Chrissie runs at him. She takes over and caresses the baby.

"Oooch Phoebe, my baby!"

Chrissie paces the room several times clutching the baby guardedly to her chest. The baby starts crying.

She sits down at the table and takes her breast out of her coat and she breastfeeds.

"We leave after breastfeed."

"Leave? You just arrived."

Joe sits in front of the carriage. He makes a sudden sharp motion to bring the horse to a stop in the fields. The horse stops.

"Damn, how could I ever forget!"

They turn back towards the house. He hits the horse. The horse goes faster. They arrive at the gates of the house.

Rick walks around the living room nervously. Chrissie sits at the table with Phoebe, breastfeeding.

"We can't stay any longer mum. We have to go before dad comes back."

"Why? The baby is fine here," says Louise.

"Mother, Chrissie isn't used to this kind of life."

They all look up when they hear the noise of the gates opening. Chrissie stands immediately with the baby and shouts hysterical.

"He's back!"

Joe enters the courtyard again. Rick embraces both Chrissie and baby and guides them to a corner in the room. He heads for the door and looks outside through the window.

"Why did he came back? To do what?"

Chrissie shivers. Rick notices it and goes back to her. He holds her close. Joe's silhouette appears at the window. The door flings open and Joe stops, silent for a moment.

"Aha, the whole family back home finally."

He steps inside.

"On my way to the village I forgot my money. But now that my family's back I'll stay home and celebrate."

Rick and Chrissie wait nervously.

"Louise why don't you take out a few bottles? I take care of the horse first."

"I make some pancakes. What a day. I still can't believe."

Joe leaves. Rick helps Chrissie to sit down with the baby and she continues the breastfeed.

"Relax Chrissie, let us eat first. You need enough food for the breast-fed anyway. Let me talk to dad later."

It's late evening. They all cheer except Chrissie. Chrissie sits on the couch with the baby in her arms. Wine glasses and empty plates remain on the table and some pancakes untouched. Louise and Rick sit at the table. Rick plays the guitar. Rick and Joe wear a paper party hat. Joe walks around the table with festoons. He spreads out additional festoons. The festoons loom over the family and the furniture. Joe takes Louise's hand and bows courteous.

"May I have the next dance, my lady?"

Louise laughs and stands up. They dance together.

The next day Joe is at a fire he created earlier. He throws several crates on the fire. He takes the ladder from the wall and chucks it on the fire. This creates more smoke.

Rick is at the window in the living room and observes that fire. Chrissie rocks the baby sitting at the table.

"He's burned the items we needed to get over and away. Talking with him is a waste of time," says Rick.

"What are we going to do next? I saw him emptying a sachet of sleeping powder in the soup. Again!"

Rick turns around and looks at her.

"In the soup?"

"Rick, that could be lethal for the baby. The chemicals that I absorb end up in the milk for the baby."

Chrissie and Rick lie down on Rick's double bed.

"At least we have each other."

Rick affectionately runs his fingers through her hair. He takes her in his arms.

"Use the condom. You know I don't want to get pregnant again."

Rick caresses her head.

"Trust me darling."

They kiss each other.

CHAPTER ELEVEN

Chrissie walks around with the baby in her arms in the courtyard. The sun shines. Rick comes out of the workroom. He has a saw in his hands. He looks at Chrissie tenderly from the doorway. The bikes lean against the courtyard wall.

"Nice day, isn't it? The fresh air is good for the baby."

"Don't talk like that. It's a prison."

"I've missed the workroom. And mother of course. And we've our bikes and things back. I asked dad to get these from the carriage."

Chrissie stops.

"Rick you don't want to stay here, do you?"

"There is no other answer. I try and make a go of it."

Rick goes to Chrissie and wants to kiss her. She pulls back. Rick heads for the workroom.

"What else can we do? Our options are limited."

Joe empties the sleeping powder sachet into the soup. It's the last sachet in the box. He throws sachet and box in the bin. Joe leaves the room and Chrissie sneaks to the bin. She takes the empty small box. She looks inside and finds a leaflet. She takes it out and unfolds it. She reads: Side effects can be nervousness, palpitations, convulsions and headaches. She hears noise. She hides the leaflet in her pocket.

Late evening Louise leaves the room. Chrissie stands before Rick and takes the leaflet out her pocket.

She unfolds the leaflet and confronts Rick. She talks to him pleadingly.

"Please read this!"

Rick rubs his eyes and yawns. Chrissie points at the leaflet.

"That's why I want to leave!"

Rick takes the leaflet and reads. Chrissie points at a certain paragraph on the leaflet.

"I don't understand what it does mean exactly."

Chrissie takes back the leaflet and reads it out.

"Side effects can be nervousness, palpitations, convulsions and headache."

Rick stands and yawns.

"You can't blame dad. He doesn't know about all these things. He can't read very well. He has dysplexia."

Chrissie's mouth falls open.

"You mean dyslexia?"

"Whatever. Let's go to bed!"

He leaves the room.

Rick is at the workbench in the workroom. Music is on. A brand new radio on batteries is on the window ledge. Chrissie observes him near the entrance. She's amazed by the scene. Rick notices over his shoulder Chrissie's arrival.

"Look what dad got us."

He goes to the radio and points at it. Rick searches randomly for other songs.

Chrissie goes away. Rick doesn't notice immediately. Then he notices she's gone. He turns around.

"Chrissie wait!"

He shakes his head and continuous his work.

It's night and dark in the empty workroom apart from the moonlight. The door flings open and a dishevelled Chrissie enters. She goes to the radio and flings it on the ground.

"Bastard!"

She stamps on the broken bits of the radio. She leaves the room.

Next morning Rick comes inside the workroom. He heads for the workbench but almost trips over the broken pieces. He takes in the damage.

"My radio!"

He runs outside

Chrissie feeds the baby in the living room. She doesn't look up when Rick enters.

"Who broke my radio?"

Chrissie doesn't respond. Rick comes closer.

"I'm the culprit!"

"You've done that? I can't believe."

Chrissie doesn't answer. Rick sits down opposite her.

"Was it an accident?"

"No. I have enough of everything! I cannot live here any longer."

"Aren't you happy with Phoebe. It's Christmas soon. I'm making a doll for Phoebe."

Later that same evening Joe, Louise, Rick and Chrissie sit at the table. Chrissie looks dishevelled. They've just finished supper. The baby sleeps in the cradle. There's an uneasy silence. Rick gets up.

"If nobody talks, I'm going to finish my carving."

Chrissie looks forlornly. Rick watches Chrissie. Chrissie sharply walks to the baby. Rick leaves the room.

Chrissie picks up the baby. Louise goes to the kitchen corner and looks after her plants. Joe watches Chrissie with that grimace on his face. Chrissie doesn't notice. Sweat on his face. He opens his mouth. He shakes his head and turns away from Chrissie. He howls. Chrissie is startled by the howl and she looks up. Joe leaves the room fast.

Rick lies on his back with his hands folded under his head. He looks at the ceiling. Chrissie lies with her back to him. Rick massages her back gently. Chrissie doesn't react. He turns to Chrissie. He takes the blankets down and watches her silhouette. Chrissie puts the blankets up again.

"No Rick."

Rick pulls back and sighs. He looks at the ceiling again.

"Why not?"

"I don't want to become pregnant again."

Rick massages her shoulders again. Chrissie stands up. She leaves the room. Rick sits up also.

"Where're you going?"

"From now on I'm going to sleep in the spare room."

Rick falls down.

"Great!"

The next day Chrissie walks around silently in the bedroom of Joe and Louise. She opens the chests of drawers and searches. She finds Joe's sleeping powder box, with the sachets. She takes it and closes the drawer. She leaves the room.

Chrissie sits on the bed in the spare bedroom. Beside her is an open packet of flour. She takes several sachets with sleeping powder out of the box. She careful rips one of the sachets. She pours the content in an empty pot. She uses a small spoon and substitutes the content of the empty sachet with flour. With a glue-stick she pastes the sachet opening. She clasps the sachet and rubs firmly across. She puts the sachet back in the box. She takes another sachet and repeats the action. The amount of powder in the pot grows.

Back in the bedroom of Joe and Louise, Chrissie goes to the drawer where she found the box with the sachets full of sleeping powder. She opens the drawer and puts the box back, now with sachets filled with flour, instead of sleeping powder.

Chrissie sits on the couch with the baby. Louise serves Joe's soup into a bowl. She opens the door.

"Joe! Your soup!"

Louise can't see Joe and goes outside. Chrissie runs fast to the table and takes a small plastic sachet with sleeping powder from her pocket. She pours the content in Joe's soup. She returns the empty sachet to her pocket and returns to the couch. Joe enters followed by Louise.

Chrissie and Rick find Joe who sits at the table and is asleep. He lies with his head on his arms and snores. Rick Chuckles.

"Who's sleeping now?"

Chrissie doesn't respond. She goes to the baby. Rick follows her.

"Why don't you say anything, asks Rick."

"Shut up Rick. Leave me alone."

"Look at yourself Chrissie. Why don't you dress up anymore?"

Chrissie turns around and shouts at him.

"Didn't you hear? Leave me alone!"

Rick leaves. Chrissie watches Joe still sleeping. She approaches him. She looks at the keys hanging at his belt.

Chrissie is warmly dressed. She walks around in the courtyard during the day with the baby in a blanket.

In the workroom, Joe looks up from the workbench. He stops working at a small table. He searches the best position to watch Chrissie through the window. Beads of sweat burst out on his forehead. He picks up another piece of wood. He holds it before him. It's as high and large as a human being. He lays the large wooden panel on the workbench. He watches Chrissie. The strange grimace appears on his face again. He goes to the workbench and take up a knife and makes a long carving in the wood panel, top to bottom. Now sweat drops from his face. He howls and his knife sinks into the wood again to carve a cross in the opposite direction. Chrissie looks up frightened when she hears the howl inside the workroom. She hurries inside the house.

Joe notices that Chrissie goes inside the house. His howl becomes stronger. He finishes the carving of the cross. He picks up the knife. He lets it fall with force in the middle of the cross, where the two lines cross. He howls again. He grabs the panel and hides it behind other panels.

The next day Louise sits in the living room with the baby on her lap. In one hand she holds a toy that tinkles. She shakes it and the baby laughs hearing.

"Phoebe, Phoebe."

Chrissie comes in from the courtyard. Chrissie's upset by the scene and walks to Louise and the baby. She takes Phoebe away.

"Come on Phoebe, time for bed"

"She didn't look tired Chrissie. She seemed to enjoy the game."

Chrissie puts the baby in cradle and cuddles her a bit.

"Children need rules and structure."

CHAPTER TWELVE

A few days later, Louise finishes the decoration of the Christmas tree. The cradle has moved to another corner, to make space for the Christmas tree. Chrissie finishes breastfeed. Rick comes in. He goes to Chrissie and the baby.

"Let me take her."

"No Rick, she just has finished her meal!"

Rick wants to take the baby. Chrissie turns the baby away from Rick. Rick shouts and tries again.

"Chrissie!"

Chrissie keeps the baby away from Rick. Rick thumps on the table with both his fists. Suddenly he has convulsions in one of his leg.

"Damn!"

He walks outside in spite of the convulsions.

Later that day, Chrissie walks inside the workroom. Her hair and clothes are very dishevelled. Rick planes wood. Chrissie goes to the wall and takes out the wood panel with the cross. She puts it before the other wood and gestures at it. Her voice tone is serious.

"What's that?"

Rick looks at it over his shoulder and laughs.

"I don't know. Must be father's work."

Chrissie talks bold.

"You don't know?"

"I've never seen at work so I can't be sure."

Rick continues his work.

"Do you ever question your father's work and actions in general?"

"The thought to question what dad does on a day-to-day basis never occurs to me."

"Is someone going to die?"

Rick laughs.

"Is someone about to cop-it, huh? Haha!"

Chrissie shouts at him.

"Doesn't that look like the top section of a coffin?"

Rick laughs ever louder. He shakes his head in disbelief.

"You've a lot of imagination. Christmas is coming and you talk about people dying."

"Is that funny?"

"Yes it is."

He continues his work and Chrissie stands alert by the door frame, her arm crossed in a defensive manner. Rick looks at her, still giggling to himself.

"What upsets you Chrissie?"

"Really?"

"You better understand that Phoebe is not just your child but my family's."

Rick faces Chrissie inches away from her head and is now menacing in his speech.

"I'm Phoebe's father. And you must understand Phoebe has also a grandfather and a grandmother."

Chrissie leaves but looks at him over her shoulder. She waits a few seconds and turns around.

"Phoebe has a grandfather and grandmother and they even don't know about her existence!"

Rick turns to the workbench again and continues his work.

"I can't help father doesn't want us to leave. But you must understand they love the baby."

"I can't believe you still defend your father."

"I'm not defending him, no. That's not the right word."

Rick shakes his head. Chrissie leaves.

In the courtyard, Chrissie walks around with the baby when she passes the workroom. She's dressed sloppy and dishevelled. She hears the sound of someone snoring.

The door of the workroom is half open. She peers inside and sees that Joe's asleep, lying on the garden chair. She looks in the direction of the house and doesn't see anyone around. She treads lightly into the workroom.

She watches the keys hanging at Joe's belt. While she holds the baby tight, she bends and tinkers at Joe's keys. She tries to take off the large key. It makes some noise. Joe stops snoring. Chrissie pulls away and heads for the door. Joe awakens. He looks with open mouth while Chrissie runs away from him.

"Chrissie!"

Chrissie disappears fast.

Chrissie walks silent but very nervous towards the drawer in the bedroom of Joe and Louise. She opens the drawer where she found the sleeping powder. She finds the box but it's empty. She puts the empty box back and closes the drawer. She leaves the room fast.

Chrissie opens her drawer in the spare bedroom. She takes up the plastic sachet where she keeps the sleeping powder. It's half empty.

"I need more."

Joe coughs when he enters the living room. He carries a crate of food and puts it on the table. Louise browses the crate.

"Could you find everything?"

"Yes, also the turkey for Christmas."

Joe takes a small bag from the crate and leaves for his bedroom. Louise takes out all the food from the crate and puts it on the table.

Chrissie lurks hidden behind the spare bedroom door managing to avoid Joe's searching eyes in his own bedroom. Joe puts ten boxes of powder in the drawer. Once the task is completed he exits the bedroom again.

Chrissie slips inside Joe's bedroom. She proceeds to the drawer with the boxes. She extracts the boxes with haste and leaves the room.

Chrissie sits on the bed again and she pours a bigger quantity of the powder from a pot into a larger plastic sachet.

It's Christmas day! All the pots boil on the stove for dinner. Louise stirs. Chrissie sits next the cradle and Phoebe with dishevelled hair and clothes. Louise goes outside. As fast as she can, Chrissie runs at the stove. She removes the plastic sachet from her jacket pocket and empties the whole lot of the powder into the pot of potatoes. She looks through the windows and spots Louise coming out of the workroom. Chrissie goes back to the baby.

Chrissie's nervous. She sits on the bed in the spare bedroom. The door is closed. Her rucksack is on the bed. She puts a large bottle of beer, cloths in the rucksack. She hides the rucksack under the bed.

She pulls the blanket from the bed and envelopes her body with it. A part of it around her shoulders. She makes a kind of a bag with her hand. She goes over it several times. She takes the bottle of beer out the rucksack again and lays it in the bag in the blanket. She walks around with it and tries out the best height and position.

It's Christmas day noon-time. Joe and Rick sit at the table with a Santa Claus hat. There're Christmas presents under the Christmas tree. Louise puts the turkey on the table. Rick plays softly songs on the guitar. Chrissie enters, dressed dishevelled.

"Ha Chrissie. There you are. We've waited for you. Some wine?" asks Joe.

Joe pours out the wine and Chrissie goes to the baby. Phoebe sleeps. Chrissie sits down at the table.

"Why didn't you dress for Christmas?"

Louise serves potatoes and vegetables. Rick cuts the turkey. They start eating. Chrissie doesn't touch the potatoes. Joe strokes Louise's arm.

"You Louise, are the ultimate Christmas dinner chef."

Louise laughs. After a while Chrissie stops eating. She drinks a bit. The others eat very slow. Rick has a convulsion at his arm and his fork falls on the floor. Louise leans back and closes her eyes. Chrissie shoves the chair and stands.

"I'm not feeling well. Please excuse me from the table."

She goes quickly to baby Phoebe scooping her into her arms. She leaves the room. Rick looks up but speaks very slow.

"What do you say love?"

Chrissie stands behind the door in the spare bedroom. Phoebe sleeps on the bed. The door's closed. She waits until all traces of human activity in the living room has receded.

In the living room, Louise leans back on her chair and she's already in a deep sleep and snores. Joe leans back also, with closed eyes. His whole body shakes. Rick lies down on the couch, with a half unwrapped bottle of champagne on his lap. He gives no sign of life. Chrissie enters. As fast as she can she takes a sharp knife and goes to Joe. She cuts the cord with the keys at his belt and goes back to the spare bedroom.

Chrissie enters the bedroom again. She takes away the blanket from the bed. She puts on her coat, scarf, hat and gloves. She wraps the blanket around her body. She takes up Phoebe and lays her carefully in the blanket that is fastened around her body. She grabs her rucksack and puts it on. She takes up the keys again and leaves the room fast.

She walks hastily outside the living room. She casts a last glance at Rick.

In the courtyard, she tries to open the locks of the gates. She trembles. It takes a while but she succeeds. She pushes one side of the gate open. She takes out the keys. She takes her bike. She walks outside with the bike.

She shuts the gate. She wants to climb on the bike but hesitates. Instead she puts the bike against the gate and locks the gates with the key. She throws away the keys. She climbs on her bike. She holds Phoebe carefully. She cycles away in the empty fields. Phoebe starts to cry.

At dusk she arrives at woodland. She stops the bike. Phoebe cries. She puts the bike against a tree. She takes her rucksack off and sits down against another tree. She caresses Phoebe.

"Phoebe, time to eat."

She breastfeeds Phoebe. While the baby drinks she takes out the bottle of beer and drinks half of it. She puts the bottle in the rucksack again. She shivers.

Chrissie cycles with Phoebe in the dark High Street of a small village. The village is absent of its populace on the streets but Christmas decorations loom from posts. The general public are inside their private spaces with their personal jubilations but illuminated to all outside by lights. She stops at the Christmas tree next the village church. She parks the bike against a bench. She watches the tree while she rocks Phoebe. She's exhausted and a mess. She shivers and heads for the church.

She enters the church. Except for a male priest the church is eerily empty. It's warm and cosy. Music is on. She sits on a bench and listens to the music. The priest notices her and walks to her.

"Merry Christmas."

She looks up blank.

"Are you alright?"

"I wanted to save my child."

The priest sits down opposite her.

"You wanted to save your child?"

"I killed the father, the grandfather and grandmother of my child."

The priest and Chrissie sit quiet. Music sounds.

PART TWO

CHAPTER ONE

Chrissie runs outside the church. She is dishevelled but holds carefully her three month old baby Phoebe in a blanket that is fastened around her body. The village Christmas tree stands next the church and Christmas decorations loom from posts but the village is absent of its populace because it is the last hours of Christmas day. The priest follows her outside. She climbs on her bike, parked against a bench.

"Come back! For the child's sake! I just called the emergencies."

She cycles away. The priest can't run that fast. He halts.

"The police want to question you."

"Question me? No way! It's Joe that wanted to kill his family. I acted in self-defence."

"They want exact locations of that house."

"I told you everything I know about the location of the house."

She cycles away. She doesn't look back anymore. Chrissie sights relieved when she enters dark country. Phoebe starts to cry.

Early morning Boxing day and Chrissie sits with Phoebe, covered with blankets, on a bench in the Victorian station. There are no other people because early morning and the odd train on boxing day. Speakers announce an early morning train to London Charing Cross. The train stops, Chrissie, Phoebe and bike enter the train.

She puts the bike against the opposite door and sinks down with Phoebe on the cosy warm seat. The train leaves.

At the same time one police car and two ambulances enter the inner court of the country house of Joe, Louise and Rick. The old horse in the stable neighs. Two police men and four health workers leave the cars. One policeman strokes the horse. The horse relaxes.

"Someone has to care for this poor fellow," says one of the policemen.

They look over the environment. The carriage for the horse stands workless before a small side-building with two windows, the workshop. The workshop is situated between an old house, the stable for the horse and the outside toilet. One policeman opens the door of the workroom and peers inside.

"Nobie's! Let's go inside the house."

The door of the main building is ajar. One police man opens the door. The other policemen keep their hand on their weapon. Near the entrance they find a large dog that appear lifeless. Around the dog are scattered turkey bones. They go inside the living room. The health workers follow him with First Aid.

Once inside a health worker kneels at the dog. He feels the body.

"His temperature is cold."

They find a living room full of wooden furniture. Next to one of the two windows, with flower-curtains, are kitchen units with a gas cooker, gas-burner plus water tank. In the middle stands a round table with six chairs. For heating there is a stove. Next to the couches, with flower-cushions, is an inactive open hearth and a very simple decorated Christmas tree. Some toys placed next to half unwrapped Christmas presents. Pieces of food from a Christmas dinner are on the table. Three people seemingly asleep, lie around the table area. The health workers run towards the casualties. Two bend over Louise, the middle-aged slovenly dressed woman, who lies on the floor. Two health workers try to revive her. The other health worker checks pulse rates of Rick, the blond, long haired attractive young man dressed in jeans. He is asleep with his head fallen on the table in a plate, half filled with Christmas dinner food. They try to put Rick upright and wipe the food from his head. One health worker goes to Joe, the sloppy dressed middle aged man who sits on a chair. He snores, with his head backwards and mouth open. The health worker takes pulse rates.

"These people need help urgently. The priest was right," says a police man.

"But the culprit fled," answers another police man

"Investigation needed before we know who caused this all. That lady said she acted in self-defence."

The police men leave the living room to inspect the other rooms of the house. The revival of Louise yields no results.

"To the hospital! Quick!"

Two health workers run outside and come back with a stretcher. They put her on the stretcher and run outside again.

"We're off now."

The policemen enter the living room again. One of the ambulances leaves the inner court.

"No other people in the house," says one of the police men.

The two other health workers give injections to Rick and Joe. Rick half opens his eyes and shuts them again. His body shivers. He again opens his eyes. He looks around bewildered.

"Chrissie! Phoebe!"

"Relax."

"What's up?"

"We took your mum to the hospital."

"Mum's in the hospital? Where is Phoebe?"

Rick tries to stand and walk over to his dad, but fails and sits down again with the help of the health worker.

"Better stay seated."

Joe stops snoring and his body trembles. He opens his eyes.

"What the hell?"

Joe stands wobbling. With his arms he swipes a plate of vegetables on the floor.

"Huuu."

The health workers put him back on the chair.

"Relax!"

Joe notices Rick sitting opposite. He shouts.

"That wife of yours! She's gone off with my grandchild."

"Dad, mum is in hospital."

"Huuu."

Joe's head drops down.

"Sir, we're taking you to the hospital."

"Phoebe! Where is Phoebe?"

Chrissie walks, with Phoebe in a blanket that is fastened around her body, in the empty early morning streets of Gravesend, a town not far from London. She heads for the cash machine. She shivers when she takes out a bank card. She puts it in the machine and types in a large sum of money. After typing the security code, a large amount of money comes out. She sights in relief. She takes out another bankcard and she starts the procedure all over. Another large amount of money pops out. She puts the money away rapidly. Phoebe starts to cry. She caresses Phoebe.

"Quiet darling. Mummy will sort everything out."

She inserts another bankcard.

Chrissie enters the bedroom of a hostel. She is loaded with food supply and puts everything on the floor. Phoebe is carefully hidden under her coat. She lays Phoebe on the bed.

"I'm happy you kept quiet. Nobody will know that you are here."

Chrissie smiles and she cuddles her baby gently. They both share a moment of joy and happiness. She holds Phoebe up in the air and turns round.

"Time for your bath darling. Mummy is going to find a way out of this. Isn't she? Yes she is!"

She lays Phoebe again on the bed. Chrissie looks out of the window into the run down street.

"However London and working in the city might be a bit of a dream for now."

In the hallway of the hospital lies Joe on a hospital stretcher with tubes in his arms. Behind him lies Rick on another stretcher with similar tubes. A few people pass by ignoring Joe and Rick.

"Damn hospital. I want my wife back"

"I want Phoebe! I want my daughter!"

"Shut up! Chrissie is the culprit. She did this to us. You know what?"

"What?"

"We get rid of these tubes and we're off."

"Nurse!"

Nobody answers his shout.

"Nurse!"

The head of a nurse pops out from the door frame of an adjacent room.

"The medics will come to you in a minute. Could you please be quiet and try to relax. We are trying to help someone who is in a worse condition."

"I want to see my wife!"

"We will come back to you as soon as we can."

The nurse returns to her duties in the adjacent room. A policeman passes by and enters into the room with the nurse. Joe tears off all the tubes coming out of his arms and stands. Rick watches him.

"What are you doing?"

"Get up. We don't need more questions from the police."

Joe tears off in a quick succession Rick's medical tubes.

"Ouch! That hurts!"

"Quiet."

Joe stands outside the room where the nurse is and listens behind the door.

"The young man asks for his wife and daughter. Where are they?"

"All we know is that she withdrew a large amount of money from an ATM in Gravesend. When can we question these two man?"

Joe goes back to Rick.

"Let's go. Chrissie is in Gravesend."

Louise's dead body lays on a slab in the hospital morgue. Joe opens the door and looks inside. He enters the small room and Rick follows. A few empty slabs and wheelchairs are around.

"Here she is. Close that door"

Joe takes the hands of Louise and kisses her on the cheek. Rick cries.

"I'll miss mum so much. We definitively had to consult a GP earlier as they said."

"Bull. They are all mad. A lot of blah blah and little help. They always promise the moon but in the end can't help at all."

"At least they could have tried. These pills you gave her, were not the right ones. Chrissie was right."

"Shut up!"

"I can't live without Phoebe. What if we can't find her?"

"I'm swearing on your mum's dead body that we'll find phoebe and Chrissie."

"Chrissie will never come to the country again. She likes the city."

"We better stay around London. We have more chances of locating them and avoiding the old Bill! We can go to the country later."

"We can't leave mum behind here."

Joe takes up his wife but falls on the floor.

"Ouch!"

Rick helps him up.

"My leg gave up. Get one of those wheelchairs. We will take care for mum properly."

Rick helps Joe loading mum in the Wheelchair.

"Quick. Open that back door."

The back door of a large building opens. Joe pushes Louise in the wheelchair outside into the back street of the small town. Rick closes the door.

CHAPTER TWO

Several days later Chrissie, wearing brand new cloths, looks sparkling. She arrives at a house in Gravesend with an announcement "For rent". She presses the bell. Terry, an attractive tall young man opens the door from the living room. He carries an empty removal box.

"Hi!"

"Hi, I saw your house is for rent?"

"It's for the house! You are godsend. Do come in and have a look around."

Terry opens the front door which comes immediately into the cosy and stylish open plan living room. Chrissie enters.

"The house is for rent furnished. You could immediately move in if you want. The renewal of my new home is finished and I move tomorrow."

"That would be great. I live in temporary accommodation with my baby daughter. We are new in town."

Chrissie walks around and admires the view from the window on a front garden.

"The agency said that a three month deposit is required?"

"Exactly."

"I'll pay everything cash."

"You seems the right kind of tenant to me. The two bedroom would suit someone like you with a small child."

She admires the open plan modern kitchen.

"No better tenant than me, I assure you. I like the house. Very sunny. All these windows looking out on greenery."

She stands still before the cable and internet connections.

"I can use these for my new online business."

"What kind of business?"

"Consultancy. I used to work for multinationals. With Phoebe it would suit me to work from home".

"Interesting. I also work sometimes from home. It saves me the commute to the city. I show you the upstairs."

She follows him towards the door.

"So you said that I can move in tomorrow?"

"That's right."

"So you said you are new in town? You don't have to feel lonely here. I'm organizing a house warming next month in my new house. You must come."

"Thanks a lot for the invite!"

The next day, the gates open and also Joe and Rick, dressed in sloppy jeans enter the inner court of an old house in a street, Gravesend area. They did some house hunting in the same area as Chrissie. There is an old side building, garage. Rick pushes the wheelchair with mum inside. Joe takes the keys out of the lock and he closes the gates with a bang.

"Our new place! Bloody expensive! Good we took all our cash with us," says Joe.

"Wow! I like it," says Rick.

"Only temporary. We'll go back to the country as soon as we can."

A wall surrounds the old house. Rick lifts up a hatch cover and notices a staircase that leads to a dark cellar.

"We don't have to use that. They said we have a fridge-freezer," explains Rick.

"We can hide mum in here," says Joe.

"That we have electricity and all these things now," says Rick.

"Maybe the electricity can help us revive mum again," says Joe.

Joe closes the hatch cover and heads for the main building. Rick follows with the wheelchair. Joe opens the door of the house with a key.

The next evening Chrissie walks around in her new rental, Terry's house, with a mop. She doesn't watch the horror movie on the television. She arranges paperwork that lies on a sideboard. She finds a photo. It's Rick standing next to her in front of an old railway carriage. She picks up the photo. The horror movie shows a murderer who tries to kill someone. Chrissie is distracted by the victim who cries and tries to save his life by fighting back. Chrissie watches the scene with the photo of Rick in her hand. Her face turns pale.

"Jesus!"

She sits on the couch with her hands on her face. She rips the photo into small pieces. Two empty bowls stand on the small table. A black one and a red one. She picks up the first small piece of photo paper and throws it in the red bowl.

"They are alive."

She takes up the next piece of paper and puts it in the black bowl.

"They are dead."

Another piece of photo paper in the red bowl.

"Alive."

Another paper in the black bowl.

"Dead."

She repeats till the last piece of photo paper. The last piece ends up in the black bowl.

"Dead!"

Chrissie stands and wanders around hysterical. She stands before the wall and bounces against it every time that she expresses the word dead.

"Dead. Maybe they are all dead and I just don't know!"

A few days later Chrissie sits at the back of a cab who follows a country road. No houses around. Phoebe is asleep next her in a baby basket. It' a cloudy day. A walled country house comes into sight, Joe's old country house.

"That's the house, there it is."

"Remote location it is for sure."

The cab stops before the house. Chrissie pops out.

"Wait for me."

"Are you sure someone living here?"

"It won't be long."

"Wait. Are you leaving that baby with me? I'm not doing child-minding!"

"Please, just a sec."

The cab driver shakes his head. Chrissie closes the door. She walks towards the wooden gate that is ajar. She opens the wooden gate outwards. The cab driver watches her entering the inner court. He takes his newspaper and starts to read.

She looks around but the inner court is empty, no dog welcomes her. The horse-drawn carriage stands without horse before a small side-building with two windows, the workroom. Chrissie quickly heads for the house. She peers through the windows. But nobody home.

She enters the living room, full of wooden furniture. The very simple decorated Christmas tree still standing. She walks around the table, where she left the whole family, after sleep inducing them. Pieces of rotten food leftovers from a Christmas dinner are on the table.

"They must be somewhere else!"

Some of Phoebe's toys placed next to half unwrapped Christmas presents. She picks up a bear and runs outside in horror.

Chrissie plops on the seat of the black cab. The driver watches her.

"I'm done. Let's go back. Please let's lose no time."

"You're the boss!"

The cab leaves.

During the night, a hand pops up on top of the wall of the graveyard and Joe's face appears. He climbs on the wall. He jumps over and lands just next to the open grave. Thunder and lightning. He takes up a wooden tree stick and makes a cross in the air. He howls like a wolf. He draws a cross on the floor. He walks towards a nearby open grave. He stands in the middle of the grave and wildly goes over the bones laying bear. He takes up a large bone and throws it in the air.

"Huuu."

Another bone in the air. More lightning and Thunder. He walks around the graves. He goes to a grave and takes the large wooden cross away. He heads for the wall. He throws the wooden cross to the other side of the wall and climbs on the wall again.

The next evening Joe and Rick plant the large wooden cross in the ground of a desolate woodland that has an expansive view. It's full moon. The empty wheelchair and a spade are the only objects around. They both stand silent and still at the makeshift grave where they have just buried wife and mother Louise.

"I'll retaliate what Chrissie did to you," says Joe.

One early spring evening Chrissie, smartly dressed, walks towards the door of a single standing charming house with a front garden. People stand before the window, dressed up with drinking glasses in their hands. Party music sounds. Chrissie presses the bell and waits. Terry opens the door.

"Hi Chrissie."

They kiss each other gently on the cheek.

"I'm so happy you could make it."

She takes a wrapped wine bottle out of her bag and hands over her present. He embraces her gently.

"Thanks. So kind of you!"

They enter the house.

The music sounds louder and people talk louder inside the house. It's full moon and a fine early spring night. The door pops open. Terry and Chrissie walk out. Terry has his arm around her waist. They laugh loudly and have drunk too much.

"It's such a lovely night. Look at that moon."

"How romantic! I'm so happy I met you."

"Are you free next Saturday evening?"

Rick walks around in the shopping mall in Gravesend High Street. There are not many people about. He notices an advert on a stand for beginners courses in electrics. He writes down the contact phone number on a piece of paper. He continues his walk.

In the evening Rick, dressed with a coat, leaves the big shopping Mall not far from Gravesend city centre. He sits down on a bench near the pond. He stares at the floor with his elbows on his knees and his hands on his face. A few other shoppers walk around. A young girl arrives.

"Someone sitting here?"

"It's yours."

She sits down and takes a fag out of her handbag. She lights the cigarette and starts smoking. Rick still stares at the floor.

"Are you waiting for someone?"

"I'm looking for my daughter and her mother."

"I see. Are they shopping?"

"No. I just don't know where they are. I haven't seen my daughter the last two years."

"Aah that's so sad."

She stands up.

"Sorry. I have to dash to work. Good luck!"

Rick nods. The girl walks away still smoking.

CHAPTER THREE

An autumn evening, a few years later, Chrissie sits by a table at the fun fair Christmas stall, next to a roller coaster. Terry and her now four year old daughter Phoebe sit next to her. They are all smartly dressed for winter with hats. They share some waffles from a plate on the table and they enjoy drinks. The crowd around cheers. Terry kisses Chrissie. Phoebe laughs. Terry holds up the plate with the waffles for Phoebe to take one.

"The last one for you Phoebe."

Phoebe nods and takes a waffle.

"She ate enough today," says Chrissie

"Just for once," explains Terry.

The roller coaster comes down fast and people scream.

"Look at that," says Terry.

Phoebe laughs.

"When is it our turn," asks Phoebe.

"We are next. Better finish our drinks," answers Terry.

They are the last to climb on the roller coaster. Ahead of them are two Santas. They sit down. Phoebe sits in the middle. Terry kisses Chrissie on her cheek and holds them both in a firm grip. The carriage immediately leaves.

"We're off," says Chrissie.

The coaster climbs.

"Watch out, we're descending fast," says Terry.

The carriage comes down fast. They laugh and have fun.

The coaster ride is almost finished. One of the two drunk Santas in front of them pushes the other Santa who collapses and almost falls out the carriage.

"Ouch! My god," says Chrissie.

Terry holds Phoebe and Chrissie close for comfort. The last moment a fatal accident is narrowly avoided involving one of the Santas. The roller coaster stops and Terry immediately jumps out. With the assistance of the fairground worker, Terry supports the drunken Santas alight from the carriage. Chrissie lifts Phoebe out of the carriage.

"Take care Phoebe."

It's hard to help walking the drunken Santas to a nearby bench.

Finally they do sit down safely. One of them immediately takes out a can of beer from his bag and drinks. They behave stupidly. Phoebe laughs.

"Haha. Why do they do that?"

"They've drunk too much," answers Chrissie.

One of the Santas starts to sing. The other falls in.

"Merry Christmas! Merry Christmas! Merry Christmas to you! Merry Christmas! Merry Christmas!"

Phoebe comes closer. Chrissie halts her.

"Stop Phoebe."

Phoebe laughs.

"Hahaha. Look! He almost falls again."

"Blimey," says Chrissie.

One of the Santas wants to come over to Phoebe. Terry prevents him.

Terry looks back at Chrissie and Phoebe. He hands over the fob of the car to Chrissie.

"Better you both get inside the car. I won't be a moment."

Phoebe and Chrissie walk in the car park towards a sleek car. Chrissie unlocks the doors of the car with a fob. Chrissie helps Phoebe into her seat in the back of the car. Just before she closes the door one of the Santas opens the front door of the car. Terry runs towards the car. The Santa flops down in the front seat. Phoebe laughs loud. Chrissie is frozen. He continuous drinking. Terry arrives.

"Terry take him away! Hurry before he vomits".

"Relax Chrissie."

Terry laughs and gently helps the Santa out the car.

"You want to take my misses away from me, don't you?"

The next day Chrissie and Phoebe decorate the Christmas tree. Phoebe is clumsy and Chrissie helps her. The open plan living room is even more cosy.

"Do it right Phoebe. Start here."

"When comes Terry?"

"Every minute. Let's finish the decoration."

"I like Terry. Daddy."

"Terry is not your daddy, he is a very good friend. I already explained. I get more Christmas crackers."

Chrissie disappears in a back room and the doorbell rings. Phoebe runs to the door.

"There he is!"

Phoebe opens the door and stares at a Santa. Santa waves at her.

"Ooch!"

Santa Claus takes out a present from his bag and gives it to Phoebe. Phoebe laughs and cheers. Chrissie walks towards the door.

"It's Santa with presents," continues Phoebe.

Chrissie stands behind Phoebe. In panic she grabs Phoebe and wants to close the door.

"Mummy it's Santa! What are you doing?"

Santa puts his foot between the door and takes off his beard. It's Terry. Phoebe laughs and cheers.

"It's Terry! Ha ha."

He steps inside. Terry kisses Phoebe and Chrissie. Phoebe jumps up and down and follows him inside.

Chrissie stands against the wall and bounces her head several times against the wall. She sighs deeply and follows them. Phoebe runs towards the tree

"Look at the tree. Mum and I have done together."

Terry admires the tree in disbelief.

"Wow. Fantastic. Well done! No better place for a Christmas party isn't it Chrissie? Why did you behave like that? Were you not expecting me?"

"Sorry I didn't recognize you at all."

"Sometimes you're a mystery to me."

"I had a bad experience in the past with a Santa."

He takes Chrissie gently in his arms and kisses her.

"Really? Sorry about that. You must tell me later the whole story. But why not enjoy the pre-Christmas vibes instead."

It's daylight and Natasha arrives in the living room of Rick's and Joe's rental in Gravesend. She is a middle aged long haired blond with high heels and short skirt, black tights and leather jacket. Her lips and her nails are dark red. The living room is very poorly decorated with an old table, four chairs and a seating corner with a couch opposite the television. Joe sits at the table. He watches Natasha walking towards him. She kisses Joe.

"Where have you been that long."

"Been to the hairdresser. Bit of a wait but I had to make myself beautiful for you."

"You look great! As always. Just in time, let's go for a walk."

Joe stands. He walks with a slight limp towards the wheelchair in the corner.

Natasha pushes Joe in the wheelchair.

"No luck with my leg playing up again but this time I'm lucky with a fantastic carer like you!"

"Shut up! You need me only a few weeks and you'll be healthy again."

"Rick works on my nerves in the end. Always drumming on about that electricity course and Christmas decorations."

"Pretty obsessed. He should think more at sex."

Joe laughs.

"You seem to know everything about it."

Just fifty metres away, Chrissie leaves a bakery and pops in Terry's car. Terry is in the driver's seat. Phoebe sits in the back. The car leaves. Joe's face changes totally. He watches mesmerized the scene.

"Stop!"

Natasha doesn't listen.

"Stop I said! Now!"

Natasha halts. A cab passes by.

"Stop that cab!"

"What's up?"

Joe stands and waves until the cab stops. He opens the door and gets in.

"Follow that car. Natasha fold that wheelchair and get in."

Natasha, looking in disbelief, folds the wheelchair and enters the cab.

"Sorry Natasha. Something of utmost importance. I need to know where these kind people are heading to. I'll explain you later."

Joe closes the door and the cab leaves.

It's dark outside but in Chrissie's living room the lights tinkle and Christmas songs all over. Phoebe sits at a table next to the Christmas tree. Before her a painting book, all with Christmas drawings waiting for colour. With a coloured pencil she gives a colour to the drawing of a Santa. She works intensely, trying out several colours Chrissie pops in from the kitchen and watches her with a satisfied look.

"Mummy, have a look at my Santa."

"Well done."

"It's daddy!"

Chrissie talks with a sharp voice.

"That's wrong Phoebe, your daddy is not Santa, I explained you."

"Shall I get a Christmas present from daddy?"

"That's not possible Phoebe."

"Can't he bring a present for me, just like the Santa?"

Phoebe turns the page of the book and a Christmas tree, waiting for colour, comes up.

"What do you think of that Christmas tree," asks Chrissie.

"I like it, but I prefer the Santa."

"And why is that?"

"Because of the presents."

"On Christmas day all presents will be under the Christmas tree."

Chrissie points at the open space under the tree in the book.

"I would like you to draw here all the presents that you want."

"Och! Haha! All the presents I want?"

"That's right Phoebe. I know you can draw very good."

Chrissie sits down in a corner of the room in front of the computer and logs in. Phoebe draws a doll. She finishes the hair, eyes and face of the doll. Once finished she grabs a scissor and another paper with figures of toys.

"Can I paste the presents?"

"Why not?"

Joe sits in the wheelchair and Natasha pushes it in the small garden next to Chrissie's house.

"Now it's dark we will have a better view."

They halt and hide behind a tree. Natasha looks around bored.

"I still do not understand why you wanted us to travel to this part of the town in the first place."

"I'll explain you later."

Joe peers through the window and looks at Phoebe, his grandchild, who pastes figures on a paper.

"At least I can have a cigarette in the meantime. I leave you here for a sec," says Natasha.

"Yeah, go ahead. I don't need that smoke. No good for my lungs."

She walks away from him towards the pavement and takes out a cigarette.

Phoebe looks up while cutting a bike. She watches Joe's head at the window.

As a result the cutting goes wrong. She notices and adapts the cutting in the right direction. She pastes the bike. She assures it sticks and stands. She takes up her paper and runs towards Chrissie while throwing another glance towards the window and Joe.

Natasha finishes her cigarette.

"Let's go to that pub again. What are you looking at? Just that Christmas tree?"

"I never saw a Christmas tree like that."

She throws her cigarette on the floor and goes over it with her foot. She walks towards Joe.

"Off we are."

"Wait a sec."

"Why are you spying on these people? I could advertise myself here for childcare. She obviously has no time for the child."

Joe looks up.

"Great idea! Couldn't have bettered it!"

"I'm always thinking at my next job. Once your foot is healed I'll be jobless."

"I treat you in the pub!"

Natasha throws a last glance through the window of Chrissie's house. She pushes the wheelchair away from the house.

"Can't wait! Such a boring suburban neighbourhood here."

"You're an angel sent from heaven."

"Why? Just because I said that?"

"Yeah. You must apply here as a child carer. I insist."

"Okay. If it makes me an angel."

"Don't tell Rick about this place. I'll explain later. Promise me."

"You're a mystery to me."

Chrissie doesn't look up first. Phoebe stands close to her mum and tries to attract her attention.

"Mummy."

"Yes."

Chrissie continues typing. Phoebe holds up her drawing. Chrissie throws a fast glance on the paper.

"Well done!"

"What present will I get from Santa?"

"We have to wait and see what the Santa will choose for you."

Phoebe nods.

"Was that the man who will bring my presents?"

"What man? What are you talking about."

"Dunno."

"What man Phoebe?"

"That man by the window?"

Phoebe points at the window.

"He stood there by the window mummy."

Chrissie stands and walks to the window. She cuddles Phoebe.

"I can't see anything. You must have dreamed."

In the pub all the tables are decorated with Elf Table Sets, Felt Chairs and Table Leg Covers. There are everywhere banners "Naughty Elves Are Living Here". A few men sit at the bar. Joe cheers wearing an elf's cap and sitting at one of the tables in a dark corner. The wheelchair sits in a corner. Natasha also wearing a cap sits on his lap. She kisses him. Naughty Christmas songs all over.

Several "Official Elf's reports lie on the table. Natasha writes down Joe's name.

"Joe has been caught being naughty. What naughty things have you done? What shall I write?"

"Ooch, one day I killed a chicken with my bare hands."

Natasha laughs.

"Is that all that you have done?"

Joe goes with his hands over her legs and feels her breasts under her blouse.

"What do you think of that? Is that naughty?"

Natasha laughs and pushes her body against Joe.

CHAPTER FOUR

The next day Rick stands on the ladder installing Christmas lights. The whole inner court of the house in Gravesend seems an electricity course practise. Christmas led rope lights, Santa Winter Wonderland lights, Acrylic Santas and snowmen with led lights, Santas in chimneys with led lights. Christmas neon effect reindeer and angel rope light. And outdoor laser lights. Joe arrives with an old motorcycle that makes a lot of noise. Rick looks up.

"Hoi! Hoi! What's up here?"

Joe stops the bike.

"That's my new bike. What do you think?"

"Is that for running circles with Natasha?"

"Ha ha. Yeah! Actually we always do circles together."

Rick concentrates on the electricity. He fixes the last parts.

"I have noticed already. I find it noisy that bike of yours."

"Well actually the destination of the bike is the country."

"The country? My god. I hope you don't want to go back to the country house."

"Well. Yeah that's what I want kiddy."

"The country again! I can't believe! I want to continue looking for Phoebe."

Rick descends the ladder. He goes towards the house. Joe parks the motorbike in a corner.

"Come on. You can't find them."

Joe stands and stretches his legs. Rick arrives at the door of the house. He turns once more towards Joe.

"What if I do?"

Rick shouts.

"Chrissie hated the place. Remember?"

"People change their minds the whole time. It's only me thinking straight," answers Joe.

"You're the straightest man in the world. No doubt," says Rick.

"Why do you wind up yourself that much?"

"You don't understand. In the country we'll never find her," says Rick.

"I might have a little surprise for you."

Rick walks again towards Joe and the bike.

"What surprise? Speak up man! Do you know where Chrissie is?"

"Tomorrow we both go somewhere you and me," explains Joe.

The next evening Joe and Rick hide behind a tree in the garden of Chrissie's house. Joe looks at the stars and Rick is mesmerized by the scene inside Chrissie's house. Phoebe runs around with Christmas crackers.

"Wow, she looks fantastic", says Rick.

"Keep quiet, someone is coming."

A car stops next the pavement and Terry comes out.

"Damn, it's a man."

Rick wants to run towards him. Joe prevents him.

"Quiet Rick."

Rick whispers now.

"Goshhhh. I have to vomit."

"Mind! Not on me."

Rick holds his hands on his face.

"What to do now?"

Terry walks towards Chrissie's house.

He knocks on the window and the door opens. He walks inside. Terry kisses Phoebe.

"Look, he kisses Phoebe. I can't stand it. I'll kill him."

"Wow, wow, shut up, I don't fancy a slaughterhouse killing. I told you already," answers Joe.

"I'm not talking butching him. If I only could electrocute that guy right now."

"You're too much a product of city life. That's what I meant by keeping away from the city. I prefer the country."

"What to do now? Damn!"

"Come on, we go home. We have seen enough for now."

Rick follows.

"I almost wished we had seen nothing today. I would like to erase this day from my life."

"No panic. For everything there is a solution," explains Joe.

A few days later Joe and Natasha arrive on the motorbike in the courtyard of Joe's old country house. The bike stops.

"Here we are," says Joe.

"Finally. I need a fag."

Natasha jumps off the bike and takes out a fag. She lights it up and briskly caresses her own arms for warmth. Joe leaves the bike. He looks around.

"I'm frozen," says Natasha.

"What do you think of my country residence?"

"Dunno, really. It's chilly."

"Let's go inside. I put the fire on."

"Let's go back before dark."

Rick and Joe are both dressed as Santa. Both wear also Santa sunglasses. They're approaching the centre of the modern shopping mall. They walk slow because of Joe's leg. It's rather quiet that time of the day.

"Let's walk to that bench. A lamely walking Santa is not a good look," says Joe.

Joe walks slowly towards a bench. Rick follows him. Joe sits.

"You just do as I told you. Never lose your act. I have seen that they always come here early Saturday morning."

"I still can't erase the image of that man from my memory," says Rick.

Rick walks nervously up and down. Joe shouts.

"Relax kid. Do sit down. I'm fed up with your childlike behavior."

Rick sits.

"They arrive now," says Joe.

Rick watches.

"Gosh what a beautiful lady she is.

"Act normal that we not attract Phoebe's attention."

Phoebe runs towards a toy shop and her mother follows.

"I could just sit here and watch them for ever."

Joe stands and stretches his leg.

"That's why I brought you here kid."

Joe sits down again and lays his head against the bench.

"Remember no sign of life," says Joe.

Phoebe runs outside the toy shop with a Christmas balloon. She loses her grip and the balloon drifts away in the direction of the two Santas, Rick and Joe. She follows the balloon and almost runs into an older woman. Chrissie follows Phoebe. Phoebe almost runs into an older woman.

"Phoebe watch out!"

Chrissie smiles at the woman.

"Sorry about that."

Phoebe continues, followed by Chrissie. Rick stands. Joe prevents him from standing.

"Remember what I told you son. Don't move a muscle."

"I just wanted to help her."

Rick sits down again and they both pretend a being half asleep. Finally

Phoebe can grab the balloon. She turns towards the Santas. They are close to Rick.

"Look mummy! The Santas are asleep."

Chrissie takes her hand. Rick leers at Chrissie behind his sunglasses.

"We have not much time Phoebe."

Chrissie and Phoebe walk away. Tears roll over Ricks face.

"Stop crying, your beard will get wet."

Rick wipes away the tears.

"I almost couldn't stop myself grabbing at her."

Chrissie and Phoebe disappear around the corner. Rick stands.

"We can't lose them again, I couldn't bear it."

Joe follows Rick.

"Not too fast."

"I would want a Christmas this year with all fairy-lights and with Chrissie and my girl."

"You are too bloody sentimental. I've been there, done that."

They turn around the corner and wait in the queue of the small mall bakery shop, just behind Chrissie and Phoebe. While Chrissie buys bread Rick changes his voice and talks to Phoebe.

"My little girl. Give me your hand."

She laughs and grabs his hand.

"What do you want from Santa?"

"A bike."

"Wow! I love cycling."

Joe pushes him and whispers in his ear.

"Let her go, the mother has seen you."

"You're a brave girl. Santa will come back to you."

Joe pushes Rick very hard now and Rick almost falls. Chrissie grabs Phoebe's hand with urgency. They walk away.

Rick is decorating Phoebe's bedroom in the Gravesend House. He hopes she will stay overnight in the near future and be reunited with her father soon. He paints a scary wild bear on the wall who plays the guitar.

A small bed for a young child sits in the centre of the room. Joe stands in the doorway.

"What are you doing now?"

"The room must be ready when Natasha will bring Phoebe here for child-minding. Now your leg is healed, she is free to do so."

"Still early days! Why that bear?"

"She always liked her teddy bear."

"Ha ha. That's not a teddy bear. That's a scary bear."

Joe walks around not lamely anymore. Rick points at the small guitar on the bed. He takes it up and start playing and behaving comically.

"She will adore the guitar."

"Shut up you. You shouldn't do such an effort. And by the way, this house is only temporary accommodation. We'll go back to where we belong."

"I can't, I need electricity. I can't live without it anymore."

"That's just imagination," answers Joe.

The next day Chrissie walks with Phoebe towards the front door of her house. She opens the door. Phoebe steps inside. Chrissie is about to go inside also, but she stops when she notices Joe. Joe walks fast and is ready to disappear around the corner. Chrissie watches intently.

"Go inside Phoebe."

Chrissie runs after Joe. She watches Joe's profile around the corner. She stands still. Phoebe stands in the doorway.

"Mummy, where are you going?"

Phoebe runs towards her mum. Chrissie takes Phoebe's hand firmly. They turn back to the house. She pushes Phoebe inside to safety.

"Let's go inside darling, you must be hungry."

During the weekend Terry and Chrissie finish a meal in a lovely country pub garden, warmly dressed in the winter sun. Terry holds her hand.

"What a lovely winter day!"

Chrissie finishes her glass of wine.

"Let's go to that desolate cabin I talked about before it gets dark."

"I'm curious what's that place about."

They both stand up and walk outside the garden, still holding each other's hands.

Chrissie and Terry sit silently in the car. Terry drives quietly. Chrissie peers nervously outside to the desolate landscape. The sun has disappeared.

"I still not understand why you wanted all of a sudden to come to this desert. We had such a nice lunch in that lovely pub. In contrast this place has such an eerie feel."

They arrive at a crossing.

"Here turn to the left. I want to be certain about something."

The car goes to the left. They notice the small wooden cabin, the hovel. Chrissie points at it.

"There it is!"

"That small cabin? I can't believe we came this far for something like that."

"Trust me, Terry."

"Is this where we are going to stay tonight?"

They arrive at the hovel and both leave the car without closing the door.

Terry stretches his arms and takes a deep breath. Chrissie walks towards the cabin.

"Stop! Time for a drink first."

He takes a flask containing coffee and hands over two plastic cups to Chrissie.

"Remember it's your idea of a day out in the country," says Terry.

"Yeah."

He comes close and kisses her. Terry pours the coffee into the cups.

"Tell me what's up darling?"

"As I said, just checking something."

"My god women can be so complicated! Is that all because you think that you have seen a relative of Phoebe?"

"Let's hope it's false alarm."

"Gosh, now it's about false alarms. You're talking in riddles."

They drink coffee and put the cups inside the car.

Chrissie and Terry opens the door of the hovel. Chrissie takes up the spade and starts digging.

"Darling, what are you doing now? We're not at the beach."

She Faster and faster. She finds a piece of cloth.

"Ooh."

"Gosh what a smell! Not promising. Let me take over that spadework," says Terry.

Terry continues the digging. Chrissie holds her handkerchief up against her nose. Terry starts to sweat and digs faster. He finds something solid.

"Blimey!"

He begins taking the sand away around the hard object. A piece of decaying corpse shows. Chrissie runs outside.

"My god!"

Terry covers the body again with the sand and lets the spade fall. He follows her outside.

Once outside Terry embraces Chrissie.

"Chrissie had you any idea we might come across a corpse?"

"It's here that Joe found me asleep that Christmas before he took me to the house."

"I guess there was no dead body yet that night you slept here. Probably it all happened afterwards."

She withdraws from Terry and walks around in circles shaking her head.

"Joe that's the grandfather of Phoebe, is that correct?" asks Terry.

"My worst nightmare! He sleep induced his family in a risky manner. This might be the result."

Terry walks to the car slowly and picks up the coffee jar.

"It's all a long time ago. Phoebe is four years old. You haven't seen anyone of that family, just now accidently coming across Phoebe's grandfather?"

Chrissie nods.

"Phoebe questions her father."

"We have to stay cool," says Terry.

Chrissie walks to passenger side of the car and opens the door.

"No thinking! Let's immediately leave this place. Nothing to do with us anymore."

"We don't know what happened, It could have been accidental death. We have to report the police," says Terry.

"No police. For Phoebe's sake, no police!" shouts Chrissie.

"From now on you both have to spend more time my place."

"We'll see about that."

"It's an order Chrissie! I care for you both. I love you. For god's sake!"

She jumps into the car and closes the door. Terry hesitates a moment and sits into the driver's seat. He closes the door and the car leaves fast.

During the night, Joe descends the stairs of the cellar in his house in Gravesend. He walks around and goes to a corner. His carpentry gear is scattered on the floor. He takes up a saw and makes the sign of a cross. He saws a piece of wood and howls wolf like. He takes the steps up and opens the hatch cover towards the inner court.

Later that night, Joe parks his motorbike with carriage in a back street. He looks around. Nobody is in the street. He opens the back door of the hospital and goes inside.

Once inside the hospital morgue, Joe picks up the corpse of a woman in a blanket. He leaves the room.

Once in the street again he starts his bike with the corpse in the carriage.

Joe drives with motorbike and carriage through the dark country.

Joe arrives with the motorbike, carriage and corpse in the courtyard of his old country house. He takes off the corpse and goes to his workroom. He opens the door. With a bang, Joe lets fall the corpse on the work bench.

CHAPTER FIVE

A few nights later, Joe arrives in the inner court of his house in Gravesend with Natasha.

"Have you already offered your child minding services to Chrissie," asks Joe.

"Thanks for reminding me! I was too busy last week. I will do that tomorrow. I promise!"

Rick switches on the electricity of his blinding Christmas decoration in the inner court.

Christmas led rope lights, Santa Winter Wonderland lights, Acrylic Santas and snowmen with led lights, Santas in chimneys with led lights. Christmas neon effect reindeer and angel rope lights and outdoor laser lights. Joe and Natasha look up.

"Wow! What do you think," asks Rick.

"Haha! Aren't you overdoing it? It lights up the whole street. It's blinding," says Joe.

"I find it all fab. Jaw-dropping and mega," says Natasha.

Rick descends from the ladder. He proudly surveys his work.

"Phoebe will adore it. If only Natasha can bring her here for child minding. Can't wait for her see it."

The next day Natasha walks towards the letter box next to the entrance door of Chrissie's house. She wants to post a letter. Chrissie suddenly opens the door and almost runs into Natasha.

"Hi," says Chrissie.

"Hi."

Natasha hands over her card to Chrissie.

"I might as well hand over my card to you instead of putting it in the letter box."

Chrissie takes the card.

"Yeah, of course! Thanks."

"I'm Natasha. I wonder if you need some childcare."

"Thanks for your offer."

"Call me anytime. I can show you reference letters."

"Great. Sorry, got to dash now! I'll contact you soon."

One evening Phoebe runs around in the front garden of Terry's house. She peers around the corner and sees a house with a lot of lights. She looks stunned.

"Ouch!"

Phoebe jumps over a small stone wall and runs on the footpath towards the house. Joe walks the opposite direction. He hides behind a wall the moment he notices Phoebe. Suddenly he notices Chrissie jumping over the same wall and running after Phoebe.

"Gosh isn't that Phoebe? I can't believe it," says Joe.

"Phoebe, come back! Where are you going?"

Phoebe looks behind and notices her mother. She halts and sits down on the floor watching quietly the Christmas decorations at Rick's house. Chrissie grabs her hand and urges her to stand up.

"Come on Phoebe. We'll go inside."

Phoebe slowly follows her mum but glances back at the lights.

"That's beautiful."

They both watch the lights.

"It's blinding."

They walk to Terry's house but Phoebe still looks back. They step over the wall and disappear. Joe follows once they disappear. He walks towards the small wall to get an idea where they are. Once arrived at the wall he tries to see as much as possible of Terry's house and inner court.

Joe enters his own house again. Rick sits before the telly, watching an old western movie. Joe turns off the telly.

"What are you doing? They just are going to shoot that guy."

He gets up to put the telly on again. Joe puts it out again.

"What are you looking at that slaughterhouse killing for."

Rick wants to stand again. Joe pushes him back into the sofa.

"What's up man? I was watching that movie. Don't you understand?"

"Luck is on our side. They are here, a few houses from here. I couldn't believe my own eyes."

"What do you mean, who's here?"

"Chrissie, Phoebe!"

Rick jumps up.

"What? Are they here?"

Joe walks towards the door.

"Follow me."

Rick follows Joe outside.

They both walk towards Terry's house. Once arrived at the wall, they both stand still and follow the movements of Chrissie and Phoebe inside the house.

"Gosh, says Rick."

"You see. In the end it all works out well in life."

Phoebe dances around the Christmas tree. Rick watches trance-like.

"Look at that! It's magical."

Joe shivers.

"It's freezing. I'm going back."

"It must be the house of that man. I could kill him with my bare hands."

"Come on, what are you talking about chap! We can cook up a tasty plan."

"I mean it."

"I need a beer for now. The solution is on our doorstep anyhow. Couldn't have been better!"

"I'll stay."

Inside Terry's house, Phoebe jumps up and down to the Christmas music, next to the Christmas tree. Chrissie lays a book on the table and leaves the room. Rick shows up just in front of the French window, standing outside. He waves at Phoebe. Phoebe looks up and laughs. She runs to the window. Rick puts his hand flat on the window. Phoebe copies him. Their hands find each other, separated by glass. Phoebe laughs. Chrissie comes in and doesn't give attention to Phoebe standing before the window. Rick withdraws. Chrissie notices Phoebe behaving strangely and approaches her.

"Why are you standing here? Why don't you play?"

"Dunno."

The next day Joe drives on his motorbike with carriage towards the hovel in the country. He stops the bike and walks towards the hovel. He throws the door open and howls like a wolf.

"Huuu."

He takes up a knife for wood from the carriage. He walks towards the hovel and places the knife into the hovel. After a few hits one of the walls falls on the ground. He tackles the other wall. It also falls down. With a few last hits the whole hovel disintegrates. He loads as much wood as possible on the carriage and leaves.

Joe is back at the cabin with the motorbike. No wood left now. Only bare sand floor.

He takes up human bones. He puts the bones in an empty plastic bag. He evens the floor with the spade.

That same evening Rick walks in the almost empty street towards Terry's house. The Christmas light coming from his own walled house flash and light up the whole street. The door of Terry's house opens and Chrissie lets out a cat.

Phoebe follows the cat outside. She is warmly dressed.

"Not too long Phoebe. Not outside the garden," warns Chrissie.

Chrissie closes the door. Rick snuck behind a wall, tries to catch the cat's attention.

"Shhhh."

Suddenly the cat notices Rick and runs towards him. Phoebe follows. The cat arrives where Rick is.

"Meow."

He picks up the cat and caresses the cat. Phoebe soon arrives at the wall and notices Rick with cat. She stops at once.

"Auuuuch."

"Is that your cat?"

"It's Minny. It's Terry's cat."

"Who is Terry?" asks Rick.

"Terry is my mum's friend. That's his house."

She points in the direction of the house.

"I see."

"Who are you?" asks Phoebe.

Rick points at the house with the Christmas decorations.

"Oooh. Is that your house?"

"Indeed it is," answers Rick.

"I don't believe you."

"Do you want to say that I'm liar?"

Phoebe stares at the lights.

"What do you think of it Phoebe?"

Phoebe looks up.

"How do you know my name?" asks Phoebe.

"I know all kind of things."

"That's like Santa. Maybe you are Santa."

The door opens and Chrissie appears. Rick hides behind the wall and he lets the cat run.

"Phoebe come back."

The cat runs towards Chrissie and Phoebe follows.

A few days later Terry, Chrissie and Phoebe go out Terry's car that has just parked street side. Phoebe immediately looks in the direction of Rick's house with the flashing lights.

"Mum, look there. I know the man who lives there."

"What man Phoebe?"

"He took up the cat. He was very kind."

"Really?"

"I like these lights," says Phoebe.

"I heard some neighbours are not happy with these blinding lights," says Terry.

"It changes the whole street, like some sort of fun fair," says Chrissie.

Terry laughs and he closes the car with the fob. They walk towards the front garden of his house.

"People said these neighbours are a bit eccentric," says Terry.

"Remember Phoebe that I told you to be careful with strangers," says Chrissie.

They enter the garden.

In the local supermarket Terry and Chrissie just check out with filled shopping bags. Terry walks towards a board on the wall. Chrissie follows.

"Let's have look if there are some ads on," says Terry.

They browse all the second hand sales offers and Terry points at a small paper.

"Childcare per hour. Call me anytime. Price to agree. Cindy."

"Maybe you should write down that number. Not easy to find a good child minder."

Chrissie takes a screen shot of it with her mobile. Terry lays his arm around her shoulder and they walk away.

"It can help giving us some just you- and-me moments from time to time," says Terry.

"Someone came to my house and gave me her card. I'll check that one first. It seemed to be someone with good references," says Chrissie.

"Really? Better not wait. We're really busy with work the whole time."

Joe pushes Natasha inside the bedroom, while embracing her. In one hand she carries her mobile. He pushes her against the wall, before the scary bear. While putting one leg between her legs, he opens her blouse. She throws her phone on Phoebe's bed. They caress each other. There is the sound of a Christmas carol coming from the phone. Natasha withdraws.

"Come on. Let it ring."

"No, wait."

She wriggles herself out of his grip and answers the phone.

"Hello, Natasha the best child minder in the world."

"Haha, says Joe."

He grabs her again but Natasha pushes him away. She gestures with her hand, making clear the importance of the phone call. Joe withdraws.

"Sure. I'll bring my reference letters. I know that street. See you there Saturday. Looking forward to meeting you."

She throws the mobile phone on the bed. Joe grabs her.

"What's up?" asks Joe.

"That was Chrissie!"

"Oh good finally! Mission totally accomplished. After putting so many cards through her letter box."

Joe kisses her all over. He pushes her towards the window.

"Guess what, says Natasha."

"Let's finish this first," says Joe.

"The interview is in a house in this same street. Must be around here somewhere."

Natasha points in the direction of Terry's house.

"I know. It's the boyfriend's house."

"Why didn't you tell?" asks Natasha."

Terry and Chrissie just finished breakfast and sit at the bar table of Terry's house. Chrissie is dressed for leisure time and Terry for the office. They both check messages on tablets. The doorbell sounds and Terry leaves the room. After a sec he is back with Natasha.

"Hi, I'm Natasha."

She walks towards Chrissie. Chrissie stands and they shake hands.

"I'm Chrissie, Phoebe's mum. Nice to meet you again. Do have a seat. Want some coffee?"

Natasha takes off her cape and throws it on a chair and also sits at the table bar. Her breast are a bit too obvious. Chrissie stares at them a short moment.

"Want some coffee?"

"Yes please. No sugar, no milk. Great place here."

"Where are you from?"

"Chatham. But I stay a lot with friends not far from here."

"That might be convenient."

Chrissie takes a fresh cup of coffee for Natasha from the machine and puts it on the table.

"Thanks."

"You said that you have some good references."

Natasha takes a few papers from her handbag and puts them before Chrissie.

"Great."

She starts reading the first letter.

"The children ask for me," says Natasha.

Natasha drinks her coffee. Terry stands and kisses Chrissie on her cheek.

"I'm off to my office. I guess you ladies can sort out everything without me."

Natasha laughs loud.

"Yeah, women between each other."

Chrissie reads the reference letter.

"We appreciate Natasha a lot. Our first impression was that of a bit of a lively lady. But our boy was depressed because of a divorce and he cheered up every time he saw Natasha. He wanted only Natasha for childcare. I recommend wholeheartedly."

"That's a lovely letter. Can you start next Saturday?"

"Your place or his place?"

"Usually during weekends we stay with Terry. Weekdays you can come to my place."

CHAPTER SIX

The sun shines. Natasha holds Phoebe's hand. They walk towards Rick's house.

"Where are we going?"

"You'll see."

"Oooh! Are we going to the house with the fairy lights?"

"Indeed. The lights will start flashing any moment. It's dark early this time of the year."

They enter the walled old house. Phoebe stops.

"Come on!"

"That man who took up Minny the cat lives here," says Phoebe.

Natasha knocks on the wood door. Rick opens.

"Look who is here! It's Phoebe," says Rick

He takes up Phoebe. She looks confused. He takes her inside.

They enter the order less living room. The telly sounds loud. Joe lies on a couch watching the news.

Rick puts Phoebe on a chair at the table.

"We might have an ice cream for you. Do you like ice cream?"

Phoebe nods. He goes to the fridge-freezer and takes out an ice cream.

He takes off the wrap-up and hands over the ice cream to Phoebe.

"Thanks."

"What a polite child," says Rick.

"You can learn from that kid. I never heard you say thank you for all what I have done for you," says Joe.

Natasha laughs and walks towards Joe. She kisses him and he takes her on his lab. Joe caresses her shoulders. Phoebe enjoys the ice cream. Rick walks around nervously.

"Let's go upstairs and have a look at your new bedroom," says Rick.

Phoebe nods and follows Rick outside the room.

Phoebe follows Rick. She climbs the stairs, one hand holding her ice cream and the other holding the rail.

Phoebe follows Rick into the bedroom and looks at the scary painting of the bear on the wall. She starts to cry.

"Mummy, where is Mummy?"

"Don't you like the bear? I painted the room for you. Look I bought you a new guitar, just like the bear in the picture".

Rick takes up the guitar from the bed and starts playing in a crazy manner. Phoebe starts to cry even harder.

"Mummy, mummy."

Phoebe walks out the room, Rick stops playing and looks up at Phoebe.

Natasha walks silently with Phoebe in the street, back to Terry's house.

"Don't tell your mum about this."

Phoebe doesn't react.

"Mouth sealed. Your mum might be angry and not allow me to come and look after you anymore. You might be left all alone in the house as a result. Do you understand?"

Phoebe nods. They arrive at the front garden and Minny the cat welcomes Phoebe. She takes up her cat and cheers up.

"See, we are home again. Nothing to cry about, sweetheart."

Phoebe nods.

A few days later Chrissie works on the computer in her own house and Phoebe watches a cartoon on the telly.

"Why do we always go to Terry's house? Why can't Natasha come here," asks Phoebe.

"Don't you like Terry's place?"

"I don't know."

"What then? You told me you had such a nice time with Natasha there?"

Chrissie stands and sits next to Phoebe on the couch.

"You must understand that during weekends Terry wants to take me out sometimes. We need time together between adults," explains Chrissie.

Phoebe lays her head against her mum.

"Mummy is going to make a nice risotto for you. How about that?"

"I like risotto. It's just that Natasha is so different."

"It's a bonus that there are all kinds of people in the world," says Chrissie.

"At school there is a boy who plays a guitar and he is very rude."

"What does he do then," asks Chrissie.

Phoebe stands and takes up a cushion and uses that as a guitar. She starts grunting musically and mimicking the scary bear playing the guitar, that Rick has painted on the wall of her future bedroom in his house.

Chrissie watches amazed.

"Phoebe what's up?"

The next week Phoebe is again in the house of Rick and Joe in Gravesend because Natasha brought here there, without the consent of Chrissie. Rick sits next to Phoebe at the table with paper for drawing. Phoebe draws a house and Rick helps.

"Here on the inner court you have to draw a horse."

"A horse! That's so hard."

She tries but fails. Rick takes over her pencil.

"I'll do it for you."

Rick draws a beautiful horse. Joe enters the room and walks to the fridge. He takes out a can of beer.

"That's a beautiful horse. I would like to have a pony. My friend from school has a pony," says Phoebe.

"We'll take you to the country one day," says Joe.

"Really," says Phoebe.

In the cellar Joe planes a piece of wood and listens to the radio.

"Date rape drugs can make you pass out. And this kind of date rape drug has no color and no taste. The victim was completely taken by surprise."

Briefly, Joe stops planing and shakes his head. He giggles. He starts to make strange grimaces and gestures the sign of the cross.

Saturday evening and Joe sits hidden behind the wall next to Terry's house. The door opens and the cat runs outside. Joe stands up and holds half a fish up.

"Come here cat. I have a job for you."

The cat goes into the direction of Joe and catches the fish. Joe plays a game with the fish, teasing the cat. He walks towards his house.

"Take it. You can have it."

He keeps teasing the cat and holds the fish from grabbing distance.

Joe arrives with the cat in the courtyard of his own house, still holding the fish. Finally the cat grabs the prey and eats the fish or what is left of it. Once the cat finishes the meal, he opens the hatch cover and pushes the cat inside the cellar with one foot.

"Come with me cat. I have more for you in the cellar. You must be thirsty."

Joe closes the hatch cover. The cat runs down the stairs and explores the cellar. Joe descends the stairs. He takes up a milk jar and puts the milk in a bowl on his workbench. He takes a small box out of his pocket and throws it in the bowl of milk. The cat jumps on the workbench and licks the milk with the now absorbed pill.

"Enjoy the milk. That's exactly what I wanted you to do. Haha."

The cat finishes the milk and runs around again, playing with a small piece of wood. After a while the cat starts running in circles faster and faster, knocking objects over in this fit. Joe follows with his eyes and turns around.

"Haha."

The cat lessens speed and collapses on the floor.

"Great, do have a nap."

Later in the evening Joe descends the stairs again and notices the cat still comatose. He takes up the half-filled milk jar and throws the content over the cat. The cat comes around.

"Meow."

She tries to stand slowly but only after a few times succeeds standing on her legs.

"You can go now. You have done the job!"

The hatch cover of the cellar lifts and the cat runs away, covered in milk. Joe climbs out. He closes the lid. Rick passes by and looks up.

"What's up? Isn't that Chrissie's cat?"

"She ended up by accident in the cellar."

"I have never seen the cat around before. Why is she that wet."

"Ooh, a kind of scientific trial."

"What do you mean," asks Rick.

Phoebe runs around in the front garden of Terry's house. Chrissie looks around.

"Phoebe when have you last seen the cat?"

"She went that way."

Phoebe points in the direction of the wall towards Joe and Rick's house. They both walk towards the wall.

"Minny, Min," says Phoebe.

"Let's go inside again. She will turn up later," says Chrissie.

"Meow."

The cat tries to jumps over the wall, dripping milk. She falls and tries to stand again without success. The cat licks the milk off her skin. Chrissie and Phoebe watch.

"What is wrong with Minny?" asks Phoebe.

Chrissie steps behind the smaller part of the wall and observes the cat.

"What happened to you? How very strange," says Chrissie.

CHAPTER SEVEN

After lunch the next day Joe and Natasha lay on the couch watching the telly.

"You know what?" asks Joe.

"What darling?"

"I was just thinking."

"Thinking about what?"

"This could be the answer to spending more time with Phoebe."

"I've managed to bring her here," answers Natasha.

"I was just thinking that you could perhaps bundle all your charms for an even better result."

"How?"

Joe stands and walks to the wardrobe.

"I'll show you."

He takes a small box out of the wardrobe and puts it on the small table next to the couch. He sits down again.

"That's it!"

Natasha opens the box and finds a small pill.

"Something to jack-up the senses," asks Natasha.

"Not exactly what you are used taking. If you only could put that in Terry's drink and seduce him."

Natasha laughs.

"That won't get Phoebe here."

"You've heard about honey traps?"

"You're wicked. However, I'm always open for an adventure. If that can help," says Natasha.

It's early evening and Natasha sits at the table with Phoebe in Terry's living room. Natasha helps Phoebe construct a walled toy country house from brick. A toy horse and dog stand in the courtyard of the toy house.

"Not like that."

Natasha demonstrates how to add another brick to the toy construction.

"I'm tired," says Phoebe.

"Why don't you go upstairs then for a nap?"

Phoebe nods and leaves the table. Natasha puts the toy house aside and clears the table. She makes herself a coffee and takes a magazine from her handbag and throws it on the table. Terry dashes in.

"Hi. Is Phoebe upstairs," asks Terry.

"She was tired after we made a toy house," explains Natasha.

She points at the house. Terry looks at it.

"What a house! God almighty! You both have a creative bent."

Natasha laughs.

Terry takes off his boots and flops on the sofa with a newspaper.

"You don't have to stay longer now. Chrissie will arrive at six. I'll look after Phoebe in the meantime."

"Okay. I'll just finish my coffee and go. Do you want a drink."

"Yeah. Thanks. I want a shot of caffeine."

"Sounds fine."

Natasha prepares his coffee from the machine.

"Milk? Sugar?"

"Milk please, no sugar."

Natasha puts milk in his coffee and promptly takes a small pill out of her handbag. She puts it in the coffee. She waits a sec until the pill has disappeared in the coffee. She hands the cup over to him.

"Thanks. I appreciate that," says Terry.

Natasha goes to the music player and browses the choice of music. Terry sips his coffee and concentrates on his paper. She chooses some soft sexy music. She locks the door of the living room quietly. She takes out her mobile and puts it on camera mode and lays it on the table. Natasha starts dancing to the sound of the music.

"I like that music," says Natasha.

Terry looks up amazed from his paper and sips from his coffee.

"Sorry that I'm concentrate on my paper. I have a lot of work waiting for me this evening," says Terry.

Terry keeps on reading and Natasha keeps on dancing. She watches Terry's behaviour secretly. While reading, Terry's head moves in motion to the beats of the music. This is for Natasha the moment to take a Christmas elf's hat out of her bag and put it on her head. Terry looks up amazed.

"What's up?"

Natasha laughs and Terry laughs also. She takes out another hat from her bag.

"I have got another one. Do you want to try it on?"

Terry starts laughing harder.

"Try? Me? No thanks".

Natasha walks behind the sofa and before he has a chance to stop her, she puts the hat on his head.

"Stop that Natasha."

"Why not? It's coming up to Christmas."

He tries to concentrate on his paper, with the hat on his head.

"Now we are both naughty elves. Once a year there are no rules," explains Natasha.

"What are you talking about?"

Natasha stands before him. She places his mobile on the small table next to the couch. She takes off her blouse. Her breast in sexy underwear pops up. Terry sits back half in horror, half in trance.

"Stop that Natasha."

His speech slurs. On the contrary she takes off her skirt and sits on his lab.

He tries to push her away but the pill has done the job and he gives in. She opens his shirt and his trousers and caresses him. Suddenly she picks up the mobile on camera mode.

"Nice smile!"

Terry looks up bedazzled at the camera. She clicks several times, taking photos of both of them half naked together on the couch.

In the hall Phoebe stands before the door of the living room but can't open it. Lighter sounds of music fill the hall. She pushes once more but the door doesn't give in.

"Mummy, mummy!"

She bounces hard on the door. After trying several times she sinks down on the floor and waits. She closes her eyes.

Terry lies half naked asleep on the couch, his elf hat still in place. The sound of the doorbell surmounts the music and he awakens. He stumbles towards the hall for the front door. By passing a mirror on one of the walls, he stops in shock noticing the state he is in.

"God almighty!"

He takes off the hat, looks at it in disbelief and throws it on the small table. He quickly arranges his clothes. He leaves the room for the hall and front door. Chrissie pops in the living room, followed by Terry. She looks over the room.

"What's that music? Feels more like a party scene."

Terry puts off the player with the fob. Chrissie takes up the elf hat and holds it up before Terry.

"Have you played naughty elves?"

"Must be from Natasha," answers Terry.

"Is Phoebe upstairs?

"She's having a nap. She was tired after making this construction with

Natasha."

He points at the toy house on the wardrobe. Chrissie looks at the toy house only briefly.

"I'll get Phoebe first."

She wants to open the door of the living room but finds out the door is blocked.

"What's that? Why is the door locked?"

Terry is speechless. Chrissie unlocks the door and a sleeping Phoebe falls into the living room.

"My god!"

Chrissie picks up Phoebe still half asleep and lies her on the couch. Terry stands next her.

"What happened Terry?"

"I'm so sorry Chrissie. It must have been Natasha. I must have fallen asleep on the couch just before she left."

"Why did she close the door?"

"Dunno, really. Maybe she wanted prevent Phoebe from waking me up. I remember saying me to her that I had a lot of work waiting tonight."

"She shouldn't do that. That you could sleep with that music on."

"I must have had a total blackout. I even don't remember putting that music on."

"You work too hard. You'll end up at the doctors."

Chrissie walks towards the wardrobe. She notices the brick toy country house and she starts trembling.

"Phoebe made that house with Natasha?"

"Yeah. Isn't she creative?"

Chrissie checks if Phoebe is still asleep and talks softly.

"That's the country house from Phoebe's father. Something is happening."

She walks around nervously with her hands on her face. Terry embraces her.

"That is just a coincidence Chrissie."

Chrissie withdraws from Terry's embrace.

"What's that smell? Have you been in a bar of something like that?"

"Chrissie! I just fell asleep!"

"We have to question Natasha about what happened," says Chrissie.

"Sure. That's what we should do."

Terry and Chrissie sit at the breakfast table, both dressed formally for work.

"I feel so much better this morning. A good night sleep has done wonders," says Terry

The doorbell sounds. Chrissie stands.

"I get that."

After a sec Chrissie is back in the living room with Natasha.

"I locked that door because I didn't want her to wake up Terry. He fell asleep on the couch just before I left," explains Natasha.

"Please don't do that again. She could have panicked."

Chrissie puts her coat and Terry's coat on a chair, ready to go.

"We both have work related meeting on Saturday morning. Happy you could make it."

"Always glad to help out," says Natasha.

"I wanted to know if that was Phoebe's idea to build that brick country house," asks Chrissie.

"Entirely. She is very good at it. She could become an architect," answers Natasha.

"That's encouraging. I'll go upstairs to say goodbye to Phoebe first."

Chrissie leaves the room. Terry concentrates on his tablet. Natasha takes her mobile out of her handbag and stands opposite Terry. She browses and opens the photo of Terry and her, half naked with elf's hats. She puts the mobile in front of Terry. He looks up from his tablet.

"Great shot of both of us. What do you think darling," asks Natasha.

Terry becomes pale and trembles being taken totally by this ruse. Chrissie appears suddenly in the living room. Natasha withdraws her mobile.

"Phoebe will come in a sec. Don't lock her out from the living room this time," says Chrissie.

Natasha laughs.

"Nothing to worry. I won't do again."

"Terry we've to dash. You said you would drop me at the conference hall," says Chrissie.

Terry stands up and puts on his coat. He follows Chrissie who puts on her coat while walking outside. Terry walks towards his car. Chrissie waits the other side of the car until he unlocks the door. He can't find the car fob in his pocket.

"Are you okay? You look very pale," asks Chrissie.

"I forgot the fob. Wait for me"

Terry hurries in again. Natasha looks up sheepishly from the table where she drinks a coffee and browses a cheap woman's magazine.

"Hey you! I'll have you prosecuted for blackmail," says Terry.

Natasha laughs.

"Do as you wish. I don't mind at all."

"What do you want from me. Is it money?"

"I could use some. Yeah. Thanks for the offer."

Terry heads for the exit. He turns around one last time and points at her. His arm trembles.

"You're going to hear from me soon."

Natasha laughs again

"You mustn't take such a position. Actually, quite looking forward to this."

"I forbid you destroying my relationship with Chrissie. I love her."

"No problem darling. I have a lover myself," says Natasha.

"For now we pay you for looking after Phoebe. Make sure she is alright. Or, we'll do much more damage than legal action."

In the evening Joe and Natasha lie lazy on the couch. Joe drinks from a can of beer. Natasha pushes the buttons of the remote control and browses the menu on the television screen.

"Now you will see!"

"Can't wait. Haha."

A last push on the remote control and the pic pops up of herself with Terry half naked, both with an elf's hat firmly on the head. Joe starts laughing loud.

"Haha! Well done. I'm so proud of you."

"You're welcome. One of my hidden talents."

He caresses her under her blouse.

"Why do you hide that lovely underwear from me."

Natasha quickly pulls out two elves hats from her bag and puts one on Joe's head and the other on her own head.

"Only once a year Christmas," says Natasha.

She stands and undresses. The sexy underwear revealed.

"Here it is. All for you. I'm always thinking, anticipating and finally initiating."

Joe takes her on his lap and they kiss.

"I've missed all these clever items in the country. I'm a lucky man."

"Everything in life has advantages and disadvantages, all balancing out over time," explains Natasha.

CHAPTER EIGHT

One evening Natasha brought Phoebe again. Phoebe runs around in the courtyard of the rental of Joe and Rick in Gravesend, while watching the flashing Christmas decorations. Joe opens the lid of the cellar and wants to climbs out. Minny the cat jumps inside.

"Where is she going?" asks Phoebe.

"Come and see," answers Joe.

Phoebe yawns.

"I'm tired."

"You can train yourself to stay awake all night."

"I wanna go to bed and sleep."

Phoebe comes closer and looks inside.

"Come and have a look."

Phoebe climbs down and walks around in the lit cellar. Joe follows.

"What are you doing here?" asks Phoebe.

"Furniture," answers Joe.

Phoebe points at one of the pieces of wood, all with crosses.

"That's a cross!"

"Yeah. I like crosses," says Joe.

"I don't like that. Minny wouldn't like it here," says Phoebe.

"Cats go everywhere where's milk."

Phoebe yawns. She takes up the cat and climbs the stairs slowly.

"I want to go home," says Phoebe.

Next evening Joe heads towards the cellar with a grimace on his face. The Christmas decoration flashes. He holds the cat firm and opens the lid. He climbs down with the cat and closes the lid.

Joe lets the cat free and she runs around in the cellar. He puts a bowl on the workbench and takes up a jar of milk. He puts the milk in the bowl. The cat climbs on the workbench. With a crude move he pushes the cat on the floor.

"Meow."

He opens a small box and takes out four tablets and throws them in the milk. He waits until they dissolve in the milk.

"Meow."

Joe puts the milk on the floor. The cat absorbs the milk. Joe looks with a satisfied grimace. He takes up a piece of wood and starts sawing it in the form of a cross. He howls loudly and manically. The cat looks up and withdraws a sec from the bowl. She continuous absorbing the milk. Another howl when he breaks the wood into four pieces. The cat has finished the milk and plays with a few utensils. The cat's movements become slow. She lies down.

"Your place is the country," says Joe.

The following day Terry is back home early. He walks towards his front garden and stops suddenly. He notices Phoebe and Natasha walking towards the neighbouring house of Rick and Joe. Neighbours he has never seen. Terry follows them. Phoebe and Natasha enter the courtyard. The gate is open. Terry enters also the courtyard.

Terry walks inside the courtyard and looks around. He hears a meowing cat and stops before the hatch cover hiding the cellar. He opens the hatch and takes out Minny.

"Meow. Meow."

The cat licks Terry's face.

"What's all this? Why are you here?"

Terry lets the cat go.

"Why don't you go home. Do never come back here."

The cat flees away. He inspects the cellar from above and notices the cross on a piece of wood.

"What the hell is that?"

He closes the hatch and walks towards the door of the house. Before he arrives the door pops open and Joe stands in the doorway.

"Hi. I'm coming for Phoebe."

Joe keeps the door wide open and makes an inviting gesture.

"Welcome. You can have a cuppa with us."

"Is Natasha inside? You know Natasha well," asks Terry.

"It's my lady. My wife died from heart disease."

"Sorry about that. We didn't know Natasha had a connection with someone close by," says Terry.

"By the way, I found my cat meowing in your cellar. How come?"

"Haha. She must have fallen in, I must have left the cover open," says Joe.

"Better take care in future," says Terry.

"You did a good thing by letting her out. Come inside," says Joe.

Terry walks inside. Joe heads for the cellar.

Terry takes in the crude interior. Phoebe sits on the couch.

"Terry," says Phoebe.

"Natasha you had no right to take Phoebe here," says Terry.

"Just friends of mine?"

"Phoebe have you been here before," asks Terry.

She nods.

"Why didn't you tell," asks Terry.

"Shut up," says Natasha.

"What game do you play Natasha?"

She looks straight into his eyes

"Life is one big game Terry. Don't you understand?"

"You know what," says Terry.

"What?"

"I'll take Phoebe home," says Terry.

"You're the boss," says Natasha.

Terry takes Phoebe's coat from the couch.

"Come Phoebe. We go home."

Phoebe stands and Terry helps her with the coat. He puts on her hat. The door flops open and Joe comes in.

"What's up? Are you leaving already," asks Joe.

Terry heads for the door with Phoebe.

"I take Phoebe to her mum", says Terry

Once in the courtyard, Terry heads for the exit. Joe follows him.

"If you're cold we might have an elf's hat for you. Haha," says Joe.

Terry doesn't look behind and walks faster, urging Phoebe to follow.

"Haha. That elf's cap is like grown on you," says Joe.

Terry and Phoebe disappear.

Once back in his house Terry receives a mobile phone call. He answers.

"Yeah it's me."

He helps Phoebe take off her coat.

"Oh god! You want me to board a plane in a couple of hours," asks Terry.

Phoebe looks up at him, confused.

"I understand. I agree that the client must be in trouble," says Terry.

"Okay I'll get a cab and go into the office first," continues Terry.

Call ended.

"I'm so sorry Phoebe but I'll have to drop you at your mum's house."

Phoebe nods.

Terry and Phoebe leave the cab and press the doorbell of Chrissie's house. Chrissie opens while talking to someone over the phone.

"Can you hold on a sec please? I come back to you."

She looks at Terry and Phoebe.

"What's up?"

"Sorry Chrissie. It all went wrong. A client is desperate on other side of the channel."

"But Natasha was meant to look after Phoebe. Wasn't she? It's exceptionally busy these days. I told you."

"Alright Chrissie. Natasha is not trustworthy. We have to look out for another child minder."

"Why? What happened?"

"I'll explain to you later. I really have to rush."

Terry leaves. Chrissie listens to her phone again.

"Thank you for holding."

Phoebe walks inside and Chrissie enter the house. Chrissie closes the door.

Phoebe sits on the couch with the child console. Chrissie walks around with the phone and browses contacts. She finds Natasha's name and clicks on it.

"Hi Natasha. How are you? Fine. Thanks. Terry mentioned there was an issue with you? What happened yesterday?"

"I see. You went with Phoebe to friends? Indeed we didn't agree about that. You know what? Let's discuss this issue later. I guess Terry has overreacted. I wonder Natasha if you could come to my house to look after Phoebe," continues Chrissie.

"Okay. I'll bring her this afternoon to where you are. I understand you have to house sit there. What's the house number?" asks Chrissie.

Natasha and Joe sit at the table and finish breakfast. Rick enters. They all wear night clothes.

"We have good news," says Joe.

Rick sits down and takes some coffee from the coffee jar.

"Speak up," says Rick.

"Hohoho. Do you speak that way to your own father?"

136

Rick drinks his coffee and takes a slice of bread.

"Shut up you. Just tell me," says Rick.

"Terry is abroad longer," says Joe.

"Is that all?"

Rick spreads his bread with butter and jam.

"Chrissie will bring Phoebe here this afternoon," says Joe.

"Wow. I have to wash my hair and dress up properly," says Rick.

"You're stupid, she can't see you. Chrissie doesn't know about us living here. We have got to hide in the cellar. You have to be patient. Your time will come."

He eats the bread.

"Disappointing," says Rick.

"I was thinking about taking Phoebe and Chrissie for a surprise Christmas party in the country," says Joe.

"Phoebe would adore that. She was so proud with the country brick house," says Rick.

"How will we get Chrissie to go out to the country again," asks Rick.

"I have a superb idea. We'll start the party here and will continue in the country. We'll need your loudspeakers and electricity knowledge," says Joe.

Rick finishes his slice of bread and goes over to the wardrobe and takes out a loudspeaker and holds it up.

"Get some Santa's here," continues Joe.

"I'll ask in the pub and find some chumps. Can't wait. We will welcome Chrissie with Christmas songs," says Rick.

Rick takes up the guitar and sings.

"Once there was a beautiful house in the country. One day a lovely lady arrived."

"Stop! She'll recognise you straight off. You can play the guitar without singing and record it as background music," says Joe.

"My electricity courses and all technical might be fruitful now. It'll help that Phoebe confuses our names," says Rick.

Rick mimics Phoebe.

"She calls me "Rei" and you "Dju"."

Rick puts the recorder on. He picks up his guitar again and plays a song without singing.

Chrissie walks with Phoebe inside the courtyard of the house of Joe and Rick in Gravesend. Even in bright daylight the Christmas lasers are flashing.

"Big surprise! It's the house with the blinding lights," says Chrissie.

"I like that," says Phoebe.

Phoebe points at the cellar;

"That's the cellar."

Chrissie stops and looks around.

"At least we'll find out who is living here now."

"Rei lives here," says Phoebe.

"Rei?"

Phoebe sits down at the table next to Natasha. Chrissie stands still wearing her coat. She takes in the uninviting decoration of the house.

"Shall we make another drawing today," asks Natasha.

Phoebe nods.

"I like drawings!"

"Glad you could bring her here," says Natasha.

"Are you living here," asks Chrissie.

"No, just friends of mine. It's convenient. So close to Terry's house."

Natasha stands up and takes paper and colour pencils from the wardrobe and puts these on the table before Phoebe. Phoebe takes a paper and pencil.

"I'm going to draw a pony!"

"Great idea! She draws very well," says Natasha.

Chrissie walks around and notices the drawing of a walled country house on a makeshift cabinet. In the courtyard of that house stand a horse and a dog. She turns a bit pale. She takes up the drawing and folds it fast, without Natasha noticing. She puts it away in her coat.

"I have to go. But if you would be so kind to bring Phoebe at Terry's house by seven? I have to feed the cat and look through his post," says Chrissie.

"Okay," answers Natasha.

Chrissie kisses Phoebe.

"Bye mum."

Chrissie leaves.

Chrissie enters Terry's living room. She puts the lights on and lays several letters on the table. The cat runs towards her. She strokes the cat and pours food and milk into the bowl for the cat. The cat licks the milk. She heads for the toy country house construction. She takes out the drawing and holds it next to the toy house. It's very similar. The doorbell rings. She folds the drawing. Chrissie leaves the room and comes back after a second with Natasha and Phoebe.

"Here she is."

"Thanks Natasha. I'll call you tomorrow when I get my work schedule sorted."

"Okay. I look forward to it. Bye."

"Bye Natasha," says Phoebe.

Natasha leaves.

Chrissie unfolds the drawing and places it before Phoebe on the table.

"Phoebe is that your drawing?"

Phoebe climbs on a chair and sits on her knees on the chair to study the drawing.

"That's mine."

"Have you done that by yourself?"

"Rei helped me."

"Rei again?" asks Chrissie.

Chrissie puts the toy country house construction on the table.

"It's the same house. Isn't it?" continues Chrissie.

Phoebe nods.

"I like that house. They have ponies there."

"Whose house is it?" asks Chrissie.

"Oohh?" asks Phoebe.

Chrissie sighs. She puts the house and drawing on the wardrobe. She picks up Terry's post.

"I sort that out at home," says Chrissie.

Phoebe strokes the cat.

"Can't we take Minny?"

"Min belongs here. Let's go."

She dims the lights and they leave.

Later that evening Chrissie talks to Terry via the internet. Terry sits in a hotel lounge in Paris.

"You really have to look for someone else for Phoebe. I don't trust Natasha at all. That house looks really strange," says Terry.

"I have seen it myself. Not my style, but it looks okay. It's also Phoebe that must adjust to another person again if we change", says Chrissie.

Terry receives an alert for a text message.

"I'll speak to you again about that. I regret being abroad just now. I must go," says Terry.

A few days later in the house of Joe and Rick, in Phoebe's bedroom, from a music box sounds hard rock and roll. Phoebe stands before the scary bear playing her guitar. Rick stands opposite her and plays on his guitar. Rick sings.

"Try to remember the lines," says Rick.

Rick sings.

"Once there was a beautiful house in the country. One day a lovely lady arrived. On Christmas day the Santa came. It was a fairy tale come true. It all ended bad one day. There was no happy ending because the beautiful lady left".

Rick stops playing.

"Now you Phoebe, repeat the lines. I know you can. You did it last week. Remember," asks Rick.

Phoebe nods.

"Now we copy a real rock concert. I'll turn up the music," says Rick.

The music is very loud and Phoebe tries to sing louder.

Phoebe sings.

"Once there was a beautiful house in the country. One day a lovely lady arrived."

That same evening in Chrissie's living room, some rock music on the radio. Phoebe watches the images of a children's book. Chrissie heads for the door.

"I'm upstairs Phoebe. I am going to take a shower."

Chrissie leaves. Phoebe walks around in the room and peers through the window. Phoebe stands and takes her guitar from a corner. She puts the radio louder and stands on the couch with the guitar. She mimes an air guitar player and tries to sing louder than the music.

"Once there was a beautiful house in the country. One day a lovely lady arrived."

She plays the guitar and mimes.

"On Christmas day the Santa came. It was a fairy tale come true. It all ended bad one day. There was no happy ending because the beautiful lady left."

More miming with the guitar. Chrissie stands in the doorway with wet hair and with a towel around her body. She quizzically watches Phoebe.

"Phoebe!"

Phoebe doesn't notice and continues playing the guitar. Chrissie goes to the radio and puts it off. Phoebe stops playing and looks up.

"What are you doing? I told you not to stand on the couch."

Phoebe sits down at once.

"Where did you learn these words?" asks Chrissie.

CHAPTER TEN

The moon shines. Joe arrives in the courtyard of his country house with a horse on a lead. He attaches the lead at the post.

The workroom of Joe is lit with a gas burner. He smacks the unconscious Minny on his workbench. He takes up a saw and keeps it in the air. He howls like a wolf and makes a cross in the air.

"Herragh! Heeragh!"

The saw drops on the animal.

Joe closes the gates of his country house and climbs on the carriage with the horse waiting. He whips the horse hard and the horse neighs.

Later that evening Joe arrives with horse and carriage in the courtyard of his house in Gravesend. He opens the gates of the side building, garage and leads horse and carriage inside.

In Gravesend the next day Joe and Rick try on the Santa clothes. Natasha helps Joe arranging the beard.

"That's better. We are well prepared for Saturday. I don't know about putting a sleeping pill in Chrissie's drink. That's a bit risky isn't," asks Natasha.

"Dad's right Natasha. There is no other way Chrissie will come to the country with us," says Rick.

"Phoebe is desperate to see our country house. We couldn't give her a better Christmas present," explains Joe.

"It might be for a good cause then, that I am a partner in crime," says Natasha.

In the evening Chrissie and Phoebe arrive in Terry's living room. Chrissie goes to the fridge and takes out the milk jar. Phoebe looks around.

"Where's Minny," asks Phoebe.

"I'll look upstairs," says Chrissie.

Phoebe walks around the room and looks in every corner of the room.

"Minny, min, where are you?"

Chrissie enters again.

"I can't find here. We have not much time. I have to take you to Natasha," says Chrissie.

A message arrives on her mobile from Terry.

"Darling I'll be back home early tomorrow morning."

"Terry is back tomorrow," says Chrissie.

She texts back to Terry.

"We are worried about Minny. We cannot find her. Can't wait to see you soon."

In the cellar Joe prepares drinks, disguised a Santa without Santa sun glasses and beard. He walks around merrily with a bottle of sparkling white wine clutched in his hand. He fills five green glasses, one red glass and one blue glass. He empties the bottle. He opens two small boxes. He takes out a pill from one of the boxes and lets it fall in the red glass. The pill sizzles in the sparkling wine to integration. He takes a second pill from the other small box and lets it drop in the blue glass.

"Hopla! Done!"

The hatch cover opens and Natasha's head pops up.

"All the Santas have arrived," says Natasha.

"Let them come down," says Joe.

He hastily puts the plate with the glasses inside a wardrobe. He opens another bottle of similar wine. The first Santa descends. The second follows.

"Welcome! Haha!"

Three Santas gather around the workbench. Joe empties another bottle of sparking white wine into five other green glasses.

"Let's have an initiating drink first. This is how we are gonna party," says Joe.

"Great! Sounds good," says one of the Santas.

Rick semi-disguised as a Santa, carrying with his hand the beard and Santa sun glasses, climbs down and almost falls.

"Haha! Watch out Rick. Santas do not fall," says Joe.

"Just nerves. That's all. I hope Chrissie hasn't forgotten," says Rick.

"Now I want you all to remember this. When I arrive in the courtyard with the glasses, just take up one of the green glasses. Just like these. The red and blue glasses are non-alcoholic. For the child," says Joe.

He keeps up his glass.

"Cheers!"

All Santas take up a glass.

"Cheers!"

"Let's repeat our songs first," says another Santa.

The moon shines. Chrissie and Phoebe arrive in the courtyard of the house of Joe and Rick in Gravesend. The moment they come in, all the Christmas laser lights flash. Chrissie is taken by surprise. Phoebe laughs. Suddenly there is loud sound of Christmas songs via loudspeakers. Natasha leaves the house and joins them.

"We have prepared a surprise- Christmas-party-special for Phoebe," announces Natasha.

"Surprise it is," answers Chrissie.

The lid of the cellar pops up. Christmas crackers come out. Phoebe laughs. Chrissie looks up in horror when the head of a Santa pops up from the hatch cover and the sound of several singing Santas emerges. Phoebe laughs.

"Haha."

A Santa climbs out. Another Santa and two more climb out. They walk around the inner court singing songs on the background loud speaker music. They circle Phoebe and Chrissie while singing. Natasha laughs and joins the circle. One of the Santas grabs Phoebe's hand.

"Come Phoebe."

"Haha, it's Rei," says Phoebe.

Phoebe dances around the inner court with the Santa. The Santa let's Phoebe go and takes Chrissie's hand, inviting her to dance. She withdraws her hand. He places his arms around her waist. Chrissie wriggles away.

"Let go. No dance for me," says Chrissie.

Chrissie takes Phoebe's hand and tries to leave the circle of Santas around them. The hatch cover lifts and the head of Joe totally disguised with the beard and Santa sunglasses pops out with a plate full of filled green glasses and one blue and red glass. He goes towards the inner circle and offers all the green glasses to the Santas and Natasha. The Santas keep singing for a while with the glasses in their hands.

Joe offers the blue glass to Chrissie and the red glass to Phoebe.

"Cheers! For Christmas," says Natasha.

They all drink. One of the Santas breaks the circle and walks towards the cellar, still singing. All the Santas follow. The first Santa opens the lid and starts to climb down. All Santas follow. The last Santa closes the lid. The music via the inner court loudspeaker stops. Chrissie is gob smacked and feels dizzy. She stumbles. Phoebe also stumbles. Natasha almost pushes Chrissie and Phoebe inside the house.

"Hey, it's cold. Let's go inside," says Natasha.

The moon has disappeared when they arrive in the courtyard of the dark country house of Joe. Joe and Natasha jump off the horse carriage. Rick sits at the back with Phoebe and Chrissie unconscious, in a blanket.

The next morning Terry arrives in his living room. He puts his luggage on the floor and walks around.

"Minny, Min."

No trace of the cat. He takes out his mobile and chooses Chrissie's number. No answer.

Terry presses the doorbell of Chrissie's house. He stands before the window and peers inside.

Nobody there. He takes out a key and walks to the door again. He opens the door and steps inside. Terry yells.

"Chrissie!"

The sun shines when Terry knocks on the gate of the house of Joe and Rick, in his own street in Gravesend.

"Somebody there?"

No answer.

In the afternoon Chrissie lies on the bed in the country house of Joe and wakes up. She sits up and looks around. She stands and bounces her head softly against the wall several times. She realizes she is in her old bedroom in the country where she was held captive a few years ago by Joe, the grandfather of Phoebe. She sits down again. She overhears Phoebe playing with Rick in the living room. She looks around the room but is unable to find her bag or mobile phone. She looks in the cupboard. She only finds some dirty towels, and matches. She takes up the matches. She hears noise of a door that opens. She puts the matches in the cupboard again. She lies down again pretending to sleep. The bedroom door opens with Rick's head appearing. He watches Chrissie on the bed and closes the door again. Chrissie stands again and picks up the matches. She lights one.

In the living room Joe, Natasha and Phoebe dance around the Christmas tree. Rick plays the guitar. Bottles of wine and empty food cans are on the table. The door opens a bit. They do not notice Chrissie watching them with a blanket thrown over her body and hiding something behind her. Suddenly the door fully opens and Chrissie comes in. She strides towards Joe sharply and with deft move throws a burning torch at him. The Christmas tree is also on fire.

"Mummy mummy," yells Phoebe.

She grabs Phoebe as fast as she can and runs outside with her. Rick and Natasha run to Joe and hurriedly pat down the flames.

Once in the courtyard, Chrissie throws a blanket over Phoebe.

"Wait here," says Chrissie.

She goes towards the horse and attaches the carriage to the horse. The horse neighs. She places Phoebe in the seat.

"I'll hurry now. I first have to open the gate," says Chrissie.

"Where is Rei?" asks Phoebe.

With a match she puts the wooden gates on fire for making a way to escape. The horse neighs even louder. She relaxes the horse with tender strokes. The gates do burn down fast. Smoke all over the place. Phoebe coughs and the horse is very restless. She fills quickly two buckets of water from the water tank intended for the horse. Chrissie throws the buckets of water towards what is left of the gates. She jumps on the carriage and they leave the courtyard with horse and carriage, followed by smoke.

Once in the fields Chrissie looks behind and notices the fire still spreading one side. She hesitates.

"Is the house going to burn down? Are the fire men going to come," asks Phoebe.

"No Phoebe. It won't spread," answers Chrissie.

She urges the horse to run faster and they do not look back anymore.

Flashing lights come from the other side and urge Chrissie to halt. Terry and two police men jump out of a police car and runs towards the horse and carriage. The other police car drives towards the house, one side burning and alight with smoke engulfing it.

"Chrissie stop! Stop," says Terry.

Chrissie halts the horse. The two police men hold the lead. Terry jumps on the carriage and embraces Chrissie and Phoebe.

PART THREE

CHAPTER ONE

One late evening, Chrissie now a good looking professional in her late thirties, sits up on her king-sized bed in her large and stylish bedroom with views across the London skyline . She wears casual but fashioney trouser and a pullover. Papers and files are spread over the bed. Another laptop is on the king-size bed. On a small table beside the bed is a small cup of green tea, and a half-eaten cheese sandwich. She talks with her daughter Phoebe, a fourteen year old brunette, via the laptop screen. Phoebe sits on her bed in the boarding school wearing her blue school uniform. She shows her mum one of her sketches of a London park.

"Well done Phoebe! But I really can't let you go to the countryside," says Chrissie.

"Mum! It's landscape drawing in the country. We can't draw that in London, why don't you get it?"

"I said no, Phoebe. There's acres of greenery just on the fringes of the City. Think of all the advantages you can take being at a residential boarding school in the centre of town."

"But Mum, I'm thinking really rural. All my friends are going to the country except me."

"We'll speak tomorrow. I'm tired honey, and I still have a ton of work to get through."

"Mum!"

"Bye, hon!"

She turns off her facetime connection and browses some spreadsheets. Images of London lofts appear. She groans. She closes her eyelids, and falls rapidly to sleep. She dreams and has a nightmare.

Chrissie, dishevelled, walks around and between the wooden furniture of the simply decorated and dark living room in the country house of Joe and Rick.

She carries her baby Phoebe in her right arm and in her left arm she holds a burning torch. She tries to open the door but can't. She screams. Joe a middle aged tall man disguised as a Santa Claus walks towards her. Joe swiftly grabs the torch and waves it close to baby Phoebe's head.

Chrissie screams.

Rick a tall young man also disguised as a Santa runs towards his father and takes away his torch.

"What the hell do you think you're playing at? Get away! It's my daughter and your granddaughter," yells Rick.

Joe opens a lid on the floor. He descends the stairs and disappears. Chrissie tries to open the door but Rick pushes her also in the cellar. Chrissie's fall ends just in front of a small table where Phoebe in boarding school uniform finishes her sketch of the London park. Santa Joe walks towards the small table with a red glass of fluid. Phoebe keeps on drawing, not bothering about Joe. Joe hands over the red glass to Phoebe. She accepts it and brings the glass towards her lips. Chrissie tries to move and prevent Joe but can't move at all. Rick arrives and plays the guitar.

"Stay and never, ever leave me again. Stay and never, ever leave me again."

"Please Stop! Stop this craziness," yells Chrissie.

Chrissie, semi-conscious, semi-groggy, flails her arms against the mattress. Some of the files fall on the floor.

"No! No!"

She knocks the cup of green tea off the bedside table and it crashes to the wooden floor. She awakens in a sudden shock and looks around in a state of disorientation. She sits quiet and watches dazzling at the London skyline.

The next evening after midnight Chrissie and Terry, leave a bar in Camden High Street and laugh loudly. They are both good looking professionals in their late thirties. Terry is dressed casual and Chrissie is quite the stylish hipster. Terry stops her and kisses her. Chrissie laughs. She takes his hand and they walk on the street jolly.

"I'm exhausted. What a night," says Chrissie.

They pass by the entrance of a restaurant. The restaurant owner pushes a young woman outside. Terry takes Chrissie closer. The woman yells.

"I worked all these hours for such a small amount of money while the beggar on the corner collects all that money."

"What a kind of woman are you, criticizing someone homeless. Go away!" says the restaurant Owner.

The restaurant owner pushes the woman away. She hits the man on his chest and withdraws.

"Bastard. Bastard!" yells the woman.

Terry and Chrissie walk faster away from the scene.

"Good heavens," says Chrissie.

They head towards a quiet residential street. They enter the smaller street. They pass by a charming house with a small front garden. It's for sale. Chrissie immediately notices the sign.

"Look! For sale! Ideal investment! What a shame that our company invests only in flats," says Chrissie.

"Chrissie darling! Do you ever stop working?"

He sits down on the small wall in front of the garden and takes Chrissie on his lap. Chrissie laughs.

"You know I am a work alcoholic!"

They kiss passionately.

"You've become a kissa-holic."

They laugh and embrace more. Terry looks back at the house.

"My London flat is small and the rent is too damn high. It isn't right for the two of us. We still don't have a proper place for spending time together properly," continues Terry.

"You're always welcome at my place," says Chrissie.

"Your penthouse is not a home, it's rather an extension of your office."

"Phoebe likes the docklands community, the vibes and arts classes. She adores," explains Chrissie.

"I know. I promised her to walk along the Thames path next time."

Terry wraps his arm around her shoulder.

"But this would be a marvellous place to celebrate Christmas together."

"Terry! Don't mention Christmas. Remember what happened."

"That was a million years ago."

"I had a horrific nightmare," says Chrissie.

Terry kisses her.

"Oh darling."

"What about a short stroll along the canal," asks Chrissie.

They walk away. Terry looks one more time back at the house. They head for the canal.

They sit down on a bench near the river. Terry checks the signal on his smart phone.

"Now you're talking work," continues Chrissie.

Chrissie wants to kiss him and he puts his mobile on the bench. They kiss each other passionately.

Suddenly a young man comes from behind and grabs Terry's mobile. Terry jumps up and runs after the man. Chrissie stands and watches the scene. Terry comes back with slumped shoulders. The thief has disappeared.

"And it was such a perfect night," says Terry.

Chrissie takes out her own smart phone.

"Relax, we track the phone down."

She browses web sites. Terry kisses her.

"Thanks for that but why not finish first what we started earlier?"

Chrissie laughs. Terry continues his kisses.

"Stop that!"

"Mmmm."

He slides his hands all over her body. He intensifies his caresses. Chrissie withdraws and laughs. She continues browsing her phone.

"I don't want to be arrested for having sex in public spaces!"

"Neither do I. That's why we need a home."

"Don't forget that I am a single mother!"

Greater London, prison. Steve, a fat middle-aged inmate, walks swiftly towards the stairs in the London prison corridor. Another big inmate attacks him and pushes him against the railing.

"You're getting on my nerves with all your good manners," says the inmate.

Steve tries to free himself.

"Shut up man," says Steve.

The inmate takes him in a more firm grip and pushes Steve's face towards the gaping depth below.

"Why don't you talk a few pegs lower," says the inmate.

Joe comes around the corner. He runs towards the scene and catches the inmates arm. He twists it around.

"Let him go mate or I get my sawing gear. I put your head on my workbench and rip your body in pieces," says Joe.

The inmate loses his grip on Steve and lets Steve go. Steve breathes heavily, regaining his posture.

"Oh. I didn't know he is one of your protégés."

Joe twists around the arm of the inmate even more.

"Argh!"

"Watch out! I know your type too well," says Joe.

The inmate succeeds escaping from Joe's grip and runs away.

Joe and Steve descend the stairs in the prison.

"I can't thank you enough man. I want to make it up to you," says Steve.

"I can't stand that one. He bothers everybody. Where did you learn your good people-skills?"

"I work in the city. I'm a property investor."

"Do you? Hahaha. All these skyscrapers. I guess it is not the first time they wanted to throw you from a higher floor."

"Hmm, actually no, nothing like that has happened to me before. I can't wait to be freed from this hell hole really. I really want to get a foot in the property business again as soon as possible."

Joe and Steve arrive downstairs and continue walking.

"The mother of my granddaughter is hiding somewhere in the city. I can't describe how my son Rick misses his daughter. If you could only help us finding her," says Joe.

"It would be an honour to help you with that mate. Next week I'm a free man again. It opens a lot of opportunities," says Steve.

"My granddaughter Phoebe must be reunited with her family as soon as possible. She grows up without knowing her birth dad."

"I understand fully. I have a son myself, I almost never see him," says Steve.

"Really? How come?"

"The mother is a bitch," says Steve.

It's a sunny Autumn day. Rick rides on his motorbike in the empty fields. He rides in the direction of a dark something in the distance. He almost arrived at the walled country house of his father Joe. The fire half destroyed the wooden gates. They blow in the wind. The moment he arrives the wind blows the gates open and he rides into the courtyard of the country home of his family.

He parks the bike and takes off his helmet. He looks around at the dishevelled place, still holding his helmet. The fire damaged the workroom and stable.

"Blimey!"

He puts the helmet on the bike and walks towards the house. The once flower patterned curtains are blackened. The fire damaged front door is ajar. He pushes it open and it falls apart.

Rick comes in the living room. The interior is also half destroyed by fire. It's a complete mess. Three dead birds lay on the floor. The wooden table and chairs are blackened and the couch lies upside down. He puts the couch up and opens the cupboard under the sink. A rat runs out just next his legs. He jumps up, startled.

It's Sunday evening and Phoebe wears her pyjama. She goes around in her walk-in drawing room in her mother's penthouse. She goes to her suitcase on the floor and arranges very carefully every piece of blue uniform inside a suitcase on the floor. She goes around and she lays a pyjama on top of the other cloths. She hesitates and lays another pyjama in the suitcase. She closes the suitcase. Phoebe plops on the king-size bed in her luxury bedroom looking out over the London skyline. The room is lit with a small lamp on a table. On the bed lie several versions of drawings of a walled country house surrounded with fields. She picks up one of them and finishes the drawing. She draws the wooden gates of the country house. A short knock on the door and Chrissie comes in. She crashes on the bed next to Phoebe.

"Time for dinner, darling."

Chrissie takes up one of Phoebe's drawings and gazes at it in amazement.

"What's that?"

"It's that house, just can't forget it."

"I told you we had a near escape from a fire in a country house when you were four years old."

"I don't remember. I told you before mum. Why is it that you never talk about my father?"

"You know that your father lives somewhere abroad and is not allowed to contact us, due to his violent family background."

"I know. It's a pity that we have no photo of him."

"I just want you to have a happy childhood."

Chrissie stands.

"In five minutes dinner. Tomorrow school again."

Chrissie leaves the room. Phoebe draws several flames that engulf the whole house.

Chrissie carries the suitcase and walks with her fourteen year old daughter Phoebe towards the gates of the semi-boarding school in London. They arrive at the gates and Chrissie hands over the suitcase to Phoebe.

"I'll drop you here. The office is waiting."

They kiss goodbye. A fourteen year old brunette Claudia runs towards them.

"Hi Claudia, says Phoebe."

"Hi! Chrissie my mum will send you an email. She wanted to talk you but couldn't wait," says Claudia.

"Great. Both of you take care now. See you on the weekend," answers Chrissie.

Three other girls join them.

"We are taking part in the drawing trip to the country. We don't see why Phoebe can't come too," asks Claudia.

"We don't understand," says one of the girls.

"We all go! Why can't Phoebe come too, asks another girl."

Chrissie turns around and leaves.

"We'll talk about that later," says Chrissie.

CHAPTER TWO

In the London prison reception room, Steve, with office suit, walks towards the table where Joe sits. Steve sits opposite Joe.

"Great to see you mate, says Joe."

"I'm having great updates for you. When will you be a free man again," asks Steve.

"Next month. Can't wait. What's up?"

"My first day at work again in the city and guess who happened to be my new colleague?"

"How to guess?"

"It was the mother of your granddaughter!"

"You met Chrissie?"

"Exactly."

"Ho! That's good news! You made my day! Thank you for that mate."

"She works for that property investment company. She earns a lot of money."

"The only place she belongs is in the country. Next to the father and grandfather of her child," says Joe.

"You must prepare a work plan. I've done my bit," says Steve.

Chrissie wears a modern dressing gown. Early morning she works out on a fitness bike in the high tech decorated large bathroom in her London penthouse. In one go she dries her hair and talks via skype to Terry. Terry at the other end of the screen eats his breakfast. He's dressed for work and sits on a bar stool in his equally superb high tech open plan kitchen in his small flat.

"When does that party begins," asks Chrissie.

"I'll pick you up at five. It is essential that we have enough quality time together."

"I know, I know. Tell me about the dress code."

"I like you just as you are. No worries."

"Ha-ha, just like this? In my dressing gown?"

"Why not? You look gorgeous. What about the weekend," asks Terry.

"Work is frantic. I'll have to make up the lost time."

"Did you see your colleague cum old boyfriend lately? The one who helped you getting a foot in the London property investment business," asks Terry.

"Jake?"

"Indeed Jake!"

"He is in Berlin most of the time. I have to go now. My hair's dry."

Chrissie switches off the hair dryer.

"You look great," says Terry.

Half an hour later Chrissie, fully dressed for the office, watches the business news on another larger flat screen while she eats a jam toast. She sits on a bar stool in the open plan, very modern, stylish kitchen. Several files, laptop, ipad all over the place. The large windows show the London docklands skyline. The doorbell rings and Chrissie watches the intercom video. She sees Jake, a fashionable but sporty build thirty something man. He carries a leather briefcase.

"Jake!"

"Hi Chrissie. I just arrived from the airport, I can drive you to the office. I have the original plans from Berlin."

"Do come up."

She pushes the intercom button. He enters after the buzz. Chrissie puts another cup under the coffee machine. Another buzz. She opens the front door of the flat. Jake comes in and he greets Chrissie with a kiss either side of her face.

"Happy to be back here. Now the project might get some serious input."

"Can't wait. Have a seat."

Jake sits down on a bar stool. Chrissie puts a cup of coffee in front of Jake.

"Do you want toast," asks Chrissie.

"No thanks for the coffee. I had breakfast on the plane."

Chrissie continues eating toast. Jake takes the plans out of his briefcase and lays them on the table.

"I show you the plans instead of the Berlin flats. I wanted you to see the plans first sight."

He unfolds the plans. Chrissie scans over the plans.

"I'm excited to see these."

She points at the terraces.

"These apartments have large terraces. That's a plus. At first glance, this is a killer deal."

"I totally agree. They'll be lovely once finished. Ideal location. Very close to the city centre and in a green environment."

"It is virtually impossible to convince Steve," says Chrissie.

"That new investor? Is he trustworthy?"

"I will not let Steve have his way and let him take over with his American projects."

"I still not understand why they want him on board," says Jake.

"You have no idea what a pain in the arse he is."

"Chrissie! Your language. You have changed so much since you were abducted. Sometimes I don't recognize you from fifteen years ago."

"Cannot turn the clock back."

"I feel guilty about what happened after we split up. That I was abroad for work and not having a clue that you were in trouble."

"We both had closure about splitting up," says Chrissie.

"I know. But still. How is it going with Terry by the way?"

"We love each other and he was there for me when I needed him most. I'll never forget," answers Chrissie.

"Yes but you don't want to settle down together."

"I'm a single mother don't forget that. It's just that it's not the right time for Terry and me to share space."

Chrissie puts her cup down and spills some coffee.

"Aha!"

Jake cleans the spoil with a napkin.

Chrissie sighs heavily and tries to relax by doing some breathing exercises.

"I'm nervous about all the work," explains Chrissie.

Jake and Chrissie arrive in the sport car outside her office block. Jake drives. They stop before the large glass Docklands office building. At that precise moment Steve leaves the office building and walks toward a waiting taxi. Chrissie leaves Jake's car and heads for the building instead. Chrissie and Steve cross each other's path. Jake's car leaves and Steve notices that the driver is Jake and not Chrissie's boyfriend, Terry.

"Morning Chrissie. I was expecting to see you in the company of Terry?"

"Not so today Steve."

"How come?"

"Actually none of your business."

Steve opens the back door of the taxi waiting for him.

"Have a nice day," says Steve.

Chrissie ignores Steve and walks inside the office building. Steve enters the taxi and slams the door.

At the same time Phoebe sits back to back with her girlfriend Claudia in Kew Gardens, London. Phoebe draws a tree. Next to her lie around drawings of exotic plants and a few small pieces of paper, teared apart. She watches the drawing and sighs. She tears the paper in pieces. She draws the same tree on another paper in her sketch book. Claudia draws another side of the garden.

"Why are you so nervous," asks Claudia.

"I'm not nervous. I just want to have things right," explains Phoebe.

In the afternoon Chrissie stands in the meeting room before a group of office people who sit around a large table, laptop, ipod in front of them. Steve is one of them. On a screen are views of a Docklands duplex apartments.

"These flats are popular with those keen on space and frontage. And we've seen no significant correction in sale prices," says Chrissie.

Another slide pops up.

"I think it's important we keep focused on London and European cities," explains Chrissie.

Chrissie detaches her laptop from the screen. The director talks.

"Thanks Chrissie. Very interesting proposals. Please Steve?"

Steve nods. He stands and takes up his computer and prepares his own projection, browsing his computer. Chrissie and three other board members walk towards the small open plan kitchen and take some coffee.

"Your attention please," says Steve.

Everybody joins the conference again. Views of a Manhattan, New York, apartment block appears. They all sit down again.

"In times when questions gripping the industry in Britain are whether prices will fall or just plateau, I do consider the American market as important," explains Steve.

Chrissie looks away and taps her leg nervously. She does some breathing exercises."

"Let's consider this New York based Manhattan loft apartments."

"Steve, did you take into consideration that union trusts are planning to invest in mainland Europe on a large scale," asks Chrissie.

"Aren't we aiming for a diversified portfolio?" answers Steve.

"What about the quality questionnaire for your Cambridge Massachusetts project?" asks Chrissie.

"Indeed, we filled out our standard quality questionnaire for the Cambridge Massachusetts project," answers Steve.

"I first wanted to know what's the outcome of that?" says Chrissie.

"You know very well that the questionnaire is not always decisive," explains Steve.

"It's very important though. You forgot to mention last time."

"The only problem was that it scored lower on neighbourhood schools and other possibilities if you're shopping strictly on price."

"That's a downside!" says Chrissie.

"But it scores very high on commuter distance to New York," answers Steve.

"I think Steve has a point. Let's continue with the presentations," says a board member.

"Okay but I'm referring to some fraudulent projects in the U.S.A. We have to be careful. We're a very trustworthy company," answers Chrissie.

"Indeed we can't afford to make bad decisions," agrees the board member.

"I agree with that. That's not the point. I always do check everything due diligence. That's my style," explains Steve.

CHAPTER THREE

It's dusk. Terry's sleek car is parked before Chrissie's apartment. Terry wears a dark blue suit. Chrissie gets in the car, she's dressed sophisticated but fashionably.

"Wow! You look gorgeous!"

He kisses her.

"We'll have to stop at a mall for the flowers."

"Chrissie! You said I could rely on it!"

"I know. I'm so sorry about this. It was such a hectic day at work."

Terry starts the car. Chrissie leans her weight against him. Terry has to stop for a car he hadn't noticed. Chrissie straightens up.

"I have to concentrate on the road, we are already late. Look at this traffic," says Terry.

Chrissie takes out her mobile and browses her mail.

"We'll manage."

"This party is very important for me. Soon they will make a decision about the funds for my new research project," says Terry.

"Oh darling that's exciting."

"The city has more opportunities. I have denied that for too long. I was engaged too much in commercial tasks in Kent," continues Terry.

Terry watches Chrissie still browsing.

"By the way are you listening to me?"

"I'm listening."

She continues browsing. Terry grabs her mobile and puts it away in her handbag. Chrissie looks outside. She points at a small shopping centre with a flower shop.

"Let's stop there!"

Terry turns the car. They stop at a flower shop.

"I trust you. A nice bunch of flowers."

Chrissie steps out and goes to the shop.

Terry gets out also. He does some stretches. He tears his suit under the right armpit, by stretching his arms.

"Damn!"

He looks at the tear. A young woman passing by, watches and laughs.

"You're not properly dressed for the Gym. That's why," says the woman.

"Damn! What shall I do now? We are on our way to party," explains Terry.

"Only keep your arm down. Nobody will notice."

Chrissie comes out of the shop with a bunch of dark flowers with yellow pollen. She notices the woman talking to Terry and gives her a dirty look. The woman walks away. She gets inside the car.

"Who's that woman?"

"She just passed by."

Chrissie slams the door. Terry gets inside the car and closes the door.

The engine starts and they leave. Chrissie watches Terry gazing at the woman who walks on the footpath.

"Terry didn't you say we are late? Let's hurry up instead of looking at women."

They sit quiet for a moment. Terry eyes the bunch of rather dark flowers Chrissie has on her lab.

"Aren't these a bit morbid?"

"Not at all, I like them very much."

Terry sighs. He relaxes and concentrates on the road. He leans forward and searches the music channels. He chooses loud psychedelic music. By leaning forward some yellow pollen come down on Terry's suit, left arm. Chrissie turns the music louder.

"I like that sound."

She leans towards Terry. This way more pollen drop down on his suit.

"I'm in the party mood already," continues Chrissie.

They arrive at a large mansion. The car follows the instructions of the livered valet on the driveway. Terry parks the car.

It's a hot early Autumn evening. Chrissie jumps out of the car and walks towards the garden party. Most people are dressed for the manor. Terry follows her hastily with the flowers and wipes some of the yellow pollen.

"Wait for me Chrissie."

He lays his arm around her. An older man and woman, Terry's boss with partner, walk towards them and they shake Terry's hand. Terry hands over the flowers to the woman.

"Congrats! Happy birthday!"

"Thanks. Special colour."

"Happy birthday," says Chrissie.

The boss holds Chrissie's hands.

"This must be your lovely girlfriend!"

"Indeed. This is Chrissie."

They walk towards the garden. A band plays jazz music in a half-open illuminated garden marquee. The boss talks to Chrissie.

"Terry informs me you are in business?"

"Property."

"Property! Sounds more exciting than being a, boring scientist ."

"We hold the sciences in high regard," answers Chrissie.

Chrissie goes with her hand over the back of Terry's left arm and tries to wipe the yellow pollen. Terry looks surprised.

"Some yellow stuff on your suit. It's probably from the flowers. I hadn't noticed."

Terry tries to remove the pollen with his right hand. By doing this the wife notices the tear under his armpit.

"What happened to your suit?"

"Sorry about that. It was a bit frantic on the road."

Chrissie laughs and holds Terry's arm down while brushing him with her hand. They arrive at the party scene.

"Chrissie, the lady of the house wants to have a chat with you later but we have to welcome some other guests," says the boss.

"You'll have to tell me all about yourself," adds the lady.

"Enjoy yourself," says the boss.

Boss and wife walk away. Terry and Chrissie find another couple. Bob, a tall attractive man and Maureen, a short dark haired woman, both in their thirties. They are dressed in sophisticated but fashionably functional attire and they hold a glass of champagne. They kiss each other.

"You must come to visit us more at the Barbican," says Bob.

"Chrissie pops in when you are at work," says Maureen.

A bit farther away, a dark haired woman in her thirties, waves at Chrissie. Chrissie and Maureen waves back.

"Look, we must say hi. We'll be back in a mo," says Chrissie.

Chrissie and Maureen head off.

"Oh, we lost them already," says Terry.

They laugh. Chrissie and Maureen walks around with a confident swagger and attracts attention from onlookers. Chrissie takes a glass of champagne from a waiter and a party snack.

"I must talk to you about our daughter's communal art projects," says Chrissie.

"They are very talented. They might become great British artists," says Maureen.

"Indeed! They both are very talented!"

They walk to the group of people but rush and Chrissie collides with a woman who almost spills Chrissie's drink.

"Sorry," says Chrissie.

"Are you all right," says the woman.

Chrissie smiles and continues. They arrive at the small group of people next. They kiss each other.

Lights are on everywhere. Several couples swing on the music. Terry and Chrissie dance together and laugh.

The next day, in the living room of the country house, Rick planes the last part of the wooden table. That part of the table is still black from the fire. He follows the beats of the loud pop music on the radio. The six chairs stand loose around, already bare. He finishes and looks over the work.

"Much better."

He wipes the floor and leaves the wood shelves in a corner. He opens a paint box with brown paint and steers the paint with a brush. He looks at the large glass photo that hangs on the wall. He puts the paint box on the floor. He goes towards the large glass photo picture that hangs on the wall. He takes a cloth and cleans the glass cover of the large photo of his daughter of four years of age who stands against a wall with a large bear. She holds a child-size guitar. He finishes the cleaning and picks up the brush from the paint box.

Rick stands in the courtyard and looks up at the sky. He stretches his arms out as if he embraces the autumnal sun. The workroom and stable are renewed. No trace anymore of the fire incident. Loud pop music blares out from the radio. He picks up a folded banner. He opens the blank banner and attaches it at the wall. He goes inside the living room and comes outside again with a brush and an almost empty dark brown paint box. He paints slowly a black letter W on the banner while still moving on the beats of the music. He adds the other letters, one after the other.

"WELCOME HOME DAD".

He proudly looks over his signage work.

Rick walks up and down before the door of the prison in greater London. It's a beautiful autumn morning. The warden unlocks the prison door allowing Joe to speedily walk out.

"I'll never come back to this place," says Joe.

"They all say that mate. Good luck now," says the warden.

Rick walks towards his father. Joe notices his son.

"Rick! Ha-ha, my own son is here. Lucky me!"

They walk towards each other. Joe hits Rick gently on his shoulder. Joe looks up in the sky.

"What a splendid day for freedom! Come on, off we go to the countryside. And I cannot wait to get there."

Walking in the streets they see a pub. Joe goes to the door.

"You said you couldn't wait to get home," asks Rick.

"I'm thinking the city is not a bad idea after all."

"Cripes! I can't believe what you are saying."

Joe opens the door of the pub. They go inside.

Joe and Rick sit at a table next the window with a glass of beer. A few people sit at the counter.

"I learned a load of things in the nick. I have some breaking news."

"What's that breaking news?"

"I became friends with Steve, a London property developer."

"Is that breaking news? What does property developer entail?"

"Are you stupid?"

"Don't insult me. It's all the result of you keeping me here in the country all my life without radio and television."

"A property developer is money maker and shaker."

Joe lifts a chair and shakes the chair up and down.

"Stop that. Will you, asks the pub owner."

Joe puts the chair on the floor.

"I don't understand. What's the point," asks Rick.

"Well I talked a lot with that bloke Steve. He said he could help us."

"How?"

"Seems Chrissie is a colleague of his."

"Chrissie?"

"Yeah! Steve found here!"

"Is she in London?"

"She made it big in the city. A real property investor and with big budgets."

Rick looks outside with slumped shoulders.

"We're not allowed to enter Chrissie's nor Phoebe's neighbourhood."

"Cheer up! Have you forgotten that your father has a solution for everything. It's a win-win situation that we know where she is. Don't you think?"

"Lucky me! What kind of language do you use these days. It's a win-win situation! Did you learn that in prison?"

"First step is that we have to dress properly for the city. That way we blend in as one of them. This way we won't be too suspicious."

Terry and his colleague Bob, both carrying a sport bag, walk in the Camden street not far from the house for sale. Terry stops at the house and points at it.

"That's it! What do you reckon?"

"It's alright!"

Bob steps over the wall and Terry follows. They walk around the house. They pear inside trough the elegant window looking past the curtains.

"It's newly decorated," says Terry.

"A more central location with outside space. Cool."

"Yeah, great isn't it. Don't think Chrissie could better this. This 'll surprise her."

The next evening Rick sits on the couch in the country house living room and tinkles softly the guitar. Joe comes in and takes off his boots.

"You know what," asks Rick.

"What? Spit it out."

"Actually I'm happier in the country."

"Ha ha. Finally you come to your senses, that your dad knows what's best."

"I couldn't not work any longer in that factory."

"What happened there?"

"I'll tell you."

Rick holds a small package before a vacuum machine. The machine seals the package with a small bang. He places the package in a large box that stands next to him. He takes up another small package that needs sealing and holds it before the machine. The factory boss, a fat middle aged man in suit walks towards him. Three metres away two of Rick's colleagues organize some filled large boxes on a worktable and watch Rick and the boss.

"We keep a record on how many boxes that you can fill every day. Do as many as you can," says the boss.

Rick continuous working, now faster. The boss walks away.

The two colleagues grin at each other.

"I'll help him a bit getting his numbers up."

"Make sure we don't want to lengthen our daily production capacity," says the other colleague.

The colleague comes next to Rick. He interrupts Rick bringing his package towards the machine. The colleague pushes a few buttons.

"This way it will work better."

The colleague leaves and Rick holds the package before the machine. The moment of sealing several flames comes out. Rick withdraws. He looks around but sees nobody. He takes up another package and holds it before the machine. Flames again.

CHAPTER FOUR

Terry and Chrissie are dressed casual and hip. Terry stands at the counter of a tiny old food shop, next to Barbican. The lady from the shop wraps some paper around a box of chocolates. Chrissie looks around at the goods. A local older woman, poorly dressed with a long grey coat, unfashionable bag and scarf, comes in and heads for the queue.

"Are you in the queue dear?"

"No," answers Chrissie.

A second local older woman, similar dressed, arrives.

"Hello, are you in the queue?"

Chrissie yells.

"No! No! I'm not in the queue."

Terry looks up.

"Chrissie!"

"Sorry. It's just nerves."

The shop lady hands over the wrapped chocolates to Terry.

"Thanks!"

He goes over to Chrissie and lays his arm around her shoulder and they leave.

They enter the Barbican Plaza. They stand still a while looking at the water party in the middle of the Plaza.

"What is wrong with you today? Just now we are going to visit our friends," asks Terry.

"I feel bad. At work it's competition. We need a stronger team."

"Maybe colleagues are jealous because of all the results you got? That's very common. I read an article lately about a social research project."

"Jealousy is not justified. I work very hard. Just think at all the benefits for the pension funds, resulting from the actions of our companies."

"Pension funds strategies have been in the media a lot, unethical investments."

"Not the ones we invest in. We ensure that our yield of profits is strategically targeted."

Later in the afternoon inside the Barbican flat Terry, Chrissie, Bob and his wife Maureen sit at the tea table by the window overlooking the city. Some spirits are also on the table. Bob and Maureen are dressed casual. The interior is nineteen eighties decor. Maureen drinks whisky and swipes in the air with the glass.

"We had a nice time in Barcelona, the weather was perfect. We met several other English couples at the hotel, who we had a strong connection with," says Maureen.

"You are very social animals," says Terry.

"What else is there in life," asks Maureen.

"We also like to mingle with all kind of people, not only with couples," says Chrissie.

"I have to admit that it has a downside. I recall a couple who were into swinging," says Bob.

They all laugh.

In the kitchen Maureen gathers some dishes. Chrissie walks around the kitchen.

"These barbican kitchens, special style. Very, very eighties."

"I would prefer a more updated kitchen but the measurements didn't fit. I'm afraid Bob won't move, he has many friends around here, all a likeminded sensibility."

"If you're ever interested in a new build with sleek kitchens, I could help with pricing. I know someone who has worked in these compact Barbican interiors. I will have a chat with him for you."

"That would be wonderful."

The next day in the waiting room of the bank office Terry sits and fidgets pensively. He's casually dressed. He changes positions a few times. He stands and walks up and down the room. Suddenly the door flings open and the bank manager appears. They shake hands.

"Thank you very much for making time for me," says Terry.

"Do come in."

Terry and the bank manager sit down opposite each other.

"This Little Red Riding Hood maisonette would be a surprise for Chrissie. I can imagine the expression of my girlfriend's face when she sets eyes on the stunning maisonette, where we can have many joyous moments together."

"Let's hope there's no wolf in Grandma's nightdress and nightcap!"

Terry laughs.

"Funny!"

"If you move in together there, it'll be easier on the mortgage."

"No, I'd like to buy the house independently."

"It may help for the mortgage terms."

Terry fidgets.

"Look, I don't have a head for business, I'm a scientist but I would like to proceed with this on my own."

"The house is expensive. It's at the higher end of the market because of the location. I would recommend that you ask her opinion before you make a big decision."

Rick, dressed with a dark blue suit, opens the curtains of a dressing room in a London shop. His own plain clothes lie on the floor and another purple new suit hangs on the hook. Joe looks at him.

"That's better!"

Rick turns towards the mirror in the dressing cabin.

"I preferred the purple suit."

"Nothing extravagant. Remember, we don't want to attract unwanted attention."

"I still don't get the point of all this palaver."

"Don't forget you're a father."

"What's the point? I don't want to end up in prison like you did and I fully abide and respect the law."

"Shut up. Do as I told you. W 'll buy that suit. We have to mix with the right kind of people to gain a basic network of contacts."

A few days later, Joe and Rick, both nicely dressed with a dark blue suit, follow Steve into a coffee shop next to a busy London city street. Joe and Rick take a window seat opposite each other. Steve goes to the counter. Rick is mesmerized by the traffic in the street.

"Wow. Look at that sport car. Blimey."

"It's kind of a circus. All that noise. I would never get used to it," says Joe.

Steve comes back with three cappuccino's.

"Thanks for that," continues Joe.

They steer the coffee and drink.

"Tell me all about Chrissie. Will you? How is she," asks Rick.

"Her daughter is in a posh boarding school," answers Steve.

"Boarding school?"

Steve nods and browses his smart phone.

"That's something like our house in the country. You have to stay inside the compound though. It protects you from the outside world. It makes a lot of sense to me really," explains Joe.

He leans back and looks into the sky, dreaming away.

"Oh shut up! Is Phoebe in the country then," asks Rick.

Steve holds his phone in front of Rick.

"That must be the address of the school. It's an inner London semi-boarding school."

Rick takes up a pen and writes down the address of the boarding school on a small piece of paper. Rick stands.

"I'm off to that boarding school."

"Sit down," says Joe.

Steve holds his phone in front of Rick. It's a photo of Chrissie speaking in a conference room. Rick sits.

"Wow! She looks gorgeous! Is she still together with that man, Terry?"

"There might be some troubles," says Steve.

Joe laughs.

"Haha Chap. Now you're talking. In life you have to focus on the opportunities."

""I'll tell you something. It was someone else who dropped her in his car at the office," says Steve.

"Who?" asks Rick.

"A business partner. The company is trying to expand in Germany," says Steve.

"Germany? Seems far to me," says Rick.

"All bull shit abroad. Isn't that excellent news she left that awful man," says Joe.

"I'm not saying she left Terry," says Steve.

Joe stands.

"Where are the gents?"

"Over there," says Steve.

Joe walks away.

Joe descends from the sleek glass stairs and arrives into the gleaming loo of the London bar. One side is for ladies. Joe looks at the sign ladies and walks to the ladies toilet doors. A lady washes her hands and notices Joe.

"You must be on the other side. You are mistaken," says the lady.

Joe looks up feigning amazement.

"Oh! I'm so sorry. I hadn't been looking."

Joe keeps staring at the lady.

"Get out, now!"

The sun shines. In Camden Terry and Chrissie walk along the street. Terry walks ahead.

"Where are we going?" asks Chrissie.

Terry walks for a while. He turns to Chrissie.

"I've a surprise for you."

"What surprise?"

"You'll find out soon enough."

"What will I find out?"

Terry stands next to Chrissie.

"Close your eyes."

"Why?"

"Chrissie trust me, close your eyes and take my hand."

Chrissie closes her eyes.

"That's better. Keep them shut."

Terry leads her around the corner and stops at the house.

"Open your eyes!"

Chrissie opens her eyes and looks at the house.

"This could be our house," says Terry.

"What do you mean?"

"It's for sale. I'm considering buying that house."

"It's a nice place indeed. But Terry you know I want to keep my independence."

"I know, I know, but we could spend many hours here just you and me. And my flat is too small and too high rent."

He takes out the keys.

"Let's go inside. I received the keys for viewing. It's newly decorated."

Chrissie walks around in the living room of the house for sale.

"It must be expensive," says Chrissie.

"You could come over as much as you can."

"It's a long way from my office."

"I know but you can always sleep in your penthouse when it's more convenient for work."

They both walk around in silence.

"Let's go upstairs, we've our own walk in wardrobe."

Chrissie looks around the bedroom, decorated to perfection. Chrissie goes to Terry and takes him in her arms.

"It's all very nice Terry but I'm not sure about this whole project."

"Why not?"

Terry kisses her tenderly and falls on the bed.

"Let's try the bed," continues Terry.

"Let me try the en suite first!"

Chrissie enters the bathroom and closes the door. Terry stretches out on the bed on his back. He takes two pillows for comfort.

Chrissie enters the bedroom again. Terry lies on the bed. Chrissie walks around the room.

"You know what?"

"What's up?" asks Terry.

"Soon I'll have to spend more time in Germany."

"How much more time?"

"I don't know yet."

"Why talk about that now. Let's relax. Come to bed."

Chrissie laughs. He takes Chrissie's hand and she falls on the bed. They laugh and embrace each other.

The next morning Rick smartly dressed walks nervously up and down before the iron gates of the boarding school entrance. He keeps an eye on the playground from time to time. A school bell sounds. Several uniformed teen girls enter the playground. Rick puts himself in a position that he can see the girls. A small group of 14 year old girls play volley with a ball. The ball rolls towards the entrance. One of the girls is Phoebe and she runs after it and picks up the ball. She catches Rick's gaze and stands still for a moment. Phoebe's girlfriend, Claudia watches Phoebe standing there quiet whilst watching Rick.

"Phoebe, hurry up. We are waiting," says Claudia.

Phoebe joins her friends again and they continue the game. They cheer. Rick gazes at the girls. Nervously he takes a small device out of his pocket and takes a photo. The girls have seen Rick and they stop their game and watch Rick.

"He took a pic of us. He's a pervert," says Claudia.

"He looks okay to me," says Phoebe.

Rick withdraws and walks away.

"He is off already," says Phoebe.

They continue playing.

A few days later Rick watches through the window Joe walking around with carpentry tools, a circular saw and a hammer. Rick takes up the photo poster of Phoebe in uniform playing in the boarding school playground. Rick hangs it opposite the picture of four year old Phoebe. He stands proud before the new photo and looks at it.

"Oh Phoebe. Wish you were here."

Joe dashes in. He walks towards the table. Rick follows his moves.

"What do you think," asks Rick.

"Think about what?"

Rick points at the photo on the wall.

"That! That! Don't you recognise your own grandchild?"

Joe looks at the photo in amazement. He stands and inspects the photo.

"Gosh! Gosh! She looks beautiful."

He stands still for a moment.

"Why didn't you show me this picture earlier?"

"I wanted to surprise you."

CHAPTER FIVE

Joe stops his motorbike in the fields. He takes off his helmet and looks around satisfied. Absence of civilization around. He unloads the contents of the carriage attached to his bike. He picks up several large pieces of wood. He puts them on the floor.

Joe walks around inside the new cabin he has constructed. He checks if the door opens and closes correctly. He tries several times.

Joe walks around outside the new hovel and checks the wall.

The next day Joe and Rick are dressed for the city. They sit on a stool at a London bar next to Steve who demonstrates a virtual reality presentation of Joe's and Rick's country house. Steve inserts a brand new kitchen into the living room of the country house.

"Wow. Would be perfect for Phoebe when she visits. She is used to the squeezed comfort of a city flat," says Joe.

"Yeah. We can do that for sure. We are skilled carpenters. Just one other thing. How will Phoebe ever come to the house," asks Rick.

"In virtual reality we can do everything. I must have that photo of your daughter somewhere that you sent me," says Steve.

He browses his computer files and the photo pops up. He inserts Phoebe's avatar and suddenly Phoebe stands in the middle of the virtual refurbished kitchen of Joe's and Rick's country house.

"Wow! That's good," says Rick.

"Ha ha ha. You know a lot of tricks. It seems that you can insert anything. Even a dead body," says Joe.

"Shut up. We don't need dead people in our house," says Rick.

"I'm thinking games! It's all about shooting people," says Joe.

"This is not a game. It's just a presentation," explains Steve.

The following evening in a suburban pub there is loud music. Joe, casually dressed talks at the counter with a middle aged lady in black dress and black shoes with high heels. The woman with Joe shifts her body and glances in another direction. Joe drops a pill in her beer.

Joe walks outside the pub followed by the lady. They both drink beer. She almost collapses and Joe holds her. Joe puts their two glasses on a table outside the pub and he walks with her around the corner. She collapses semi-unconscious in his arms. He drags her towards a few trees. He lays her in the carriage of his motorbike. He covers the carriage. He starts the engine and leaves.

Four half constructed wood kitchen wall cabinets stand in the middle of the work room in the country house of Joe. The photo of Phoebe, boarding school playground, stands up on the workbench. Joe stands before the workbench and looks dishevelled. All grimaces on his face. He looks up at the photo of Phoebe while cleaning dark blood stains on the workbench with a cloth. He cleans a sharp knife also with blood. He throws away the blooded cloths in a plastic bag and closes off the plastic bag. He goes towards a wall and hides the body of the lady in a sealed transparent plastic wrap filled with blood behind the wood panels. The lady wears a black dress, black shoes with high heels. There is a sponge inside the blooded area around her heart. Suddenly the door flings open and Rick stands in the doorway.

"Morning. What's up? You came home very late last night," says Rick.

Joe turns towards Rick. He forces his face into a charming smile. All grimaces disappear. He takes up a fresh cloth.

"Ha ha ha. I just was about to clean Phoebe's photo."

"No you were not."

Joe wipes the photo thoroughly. Rick watches his moves. Joe throws the cloth aside and takes up a half empty bottle of wine.

"Time for a break. After that I will finish off our new kitchen cabinets."

Joe assembles two dirty glasses from the window sill. He opens the bottle and fills the two glasses. Rick eyes Phoebe's photo.

"What a beautiful child!"

Joe drops two pills in Rick's glass, without Rick noticing. He hands over the glass to Rick and they cheer.

It's night. Joe arrives with the motorbike with carriage at the hovel. He stops the bike hundred metres from the hovel and leaves the lights on. He off-loads the dead human body of the lady with black cloths in a sealed plastic wrap filled with blood. He takes a shovel from the bike carriage. He starts to dig a trench the size of the body. He digs quickly. Sweat beats form on his face. After enough digging he opens the plastic bag and throws the dead body into the pit. A black shoe with high heels falls outside the pit. He covers the pit with sand. Before finishing he notices the lost shoe and he adds it. He continues covering the pit. He pours some petrol on the plastic bag to get it ignited with fire and goes back to his bike and reloads the shovel. He leaves.

The following day Terry, fashionable dressed, enters a coffee house near Russel Square. A twenty something appealing and amiable, dark haired, waitress greets him.

"Hi, how are you?"

"Not too bad. And you?"

"I'm fine. A cappuccino for you?"

"Cool. You've a good memory."

The waitress makes the coffee.

"I would like to see more of my girlfriend these days. She's very busy at work in her office," continues Terry.

"You can always pop your head into her office, can't you?"

She gives him the drink and he pays.

"Thanks. I appreciate the advice and for the coffee This coffee will revive me!"

At the investment company that same evening, Jake and Chrissie sit next each other on the sofa, before the large windows, in the lounge area of Chrissie's office. There are leftovers from delivered food on the table and soft drinks. They study the plans of Berlin flats.

"Is this the duplex you mentioned," asks Chrissie.

"Indeed it's very good on the price-quality side."

"Thanks for your help Jake. It means a lot to me. I'll have to come to Berlin in person anyway."

Jake lays his hand on an arm.

"It's a pity I have to leave soon."

Downstairs Terry enters the hall of a large glass office building of the investment company. He goes to the lift.

Once in the lift Terry pushes the tenth floor button. From the glass lift he admires the London skyline. Once arrived he steps out.

Terry goes to the desk of the secretary on the tenth floor. It's empty. Steve, loaded up with files, passes by and looks surprised.

"Hi Terry, Chrissie's in her office."

"Isn't the secretary around? I can't disturb Chrissie unannounced."

Steve almost disappears around the corner. Then he looks back.

"Of course you can, don't bother."

Steve smiles in a forced manner and disappears. Terry knocks at Chrissie's office door. He waits. No answer. He walks around for a while in the corridor. He knocks again. Again, no answer. Steve arrives, without files. Steve slams open the door of Chrissie's office and leaves.

"Just go in," says Steve.

Terry sees Chrissie in office dress enjoying a soft drink with Jake's hand on her arm. Terry holds the door-latch. He throws the door fully open. The door hits the wall with a bang. Chrissie looks up and sees him.

"Terry!"

Terry runs away. She hastily runs towards the door. Terry disappears in the central hallway.

Terry enters the glass elevator again. Chrissie pushes the buttons but it's too late. The doors close together. She sees Terry going down and yells at him.

"Terry let me explain. It's not what it looks like!"

Chrissie runs towards the other glass elevator and pushes nervously the button frantically. The elevator arrives. She jumps in.

Chrissie presses the ground floor button of the second elevator. She watches Terry going further down. The second elevator stops with a shock at the seventh floor. The doors opens and a young man steps inside. He stands with his back facing her. Chrissie pushes the button for closing the door with one hand. This way she prohibits another manager from entering.

"Sorry, an emergency!"

The door closes again. She jumps from one side to the other. She leans with her front body towards the glass. She follows the progress of the other elevator. She sees Terry's elevator arriving, ground level. She bounces against the glass wall without really touching the glass.

Once downstairs Chrissie leaves the glass lift and runs towards the exit. She notices Terry jumping into his car in the adjacent street.

Chrissie runs towards his car. Both her hands hit the back of his car.

"Stop!"

Too late. The car leaves. Chrissie runs towards a waiting taxi. She opens the door and gets in.

Chrissie leans towards the driver of the taxi. She points at Terry's car.

"Please, follow that car. Quick!"

The taxi follows Terry's car.

"Faster! Don't lose the car."

The taxi speeds up.

After a while another car hits him from aside and there is a collision.

The taxi stops. Chrissie falls forward with a shock. She looks dumbfounded and dazed. The driver leaves the car

The taxi has left and Chrissie stands on the footpath of a London street. She has no coat and shivers. She searches a number on her mobile and dials.

"Hi Maureen. I wonder if you are in the neighbourhood. Could you pick me up perhaps? Kind of emergency."

A van arrives and stops before Chrissie who stands on the pavement.

Maureen steps out from the passenger seat. The driver and another removal man wait inside the van.

"Here you are? What happened," asks Maureen.

"It went wrong!"

"Come along. The driver can't wait. I'm on my way to my sister's house. Tell me everything inside."

Terry walks fast in a dark London street, he almost crashes into a young couple.

"Watch out!"

Terry doesn't notice and walks on. He avoids falling over a rubbish bag. He reaches a quiet corner next to the Thames. He kicks an empty can.

"Damn Chrissie!"

He leans over the rail next the Thames.

Back in his small flat Terry comes in the bedroom, dishevelled. He throws himself on the bed fully clothed. A short moment later he jumps up. He takes an old plastic high street shopping bag and goes to the walk in wardrobe. He notices the nightclothes of Chrissie and throws them in the bin.

In the bathroom he goes to Chrissie's separate fitted wash-basin. He throws the toothbrush, paste and other small items in the bag.

He leaves the bag in the bedroom and lays on the bed again. His mobile rings but he doesn't answer. After a few rings the mobile is quiet. He gets up. He walks around aimlessly. He goes to the bathroom again.

He takes off his clothes and takes a shower. He goes over his face and hair with his hands.

The van, with Maureen and Chrissie stops before an Edwardian house with a front garden. They bang the horn and try to park in an aggressive manner before another van. Maureen steps out. She carries a large empty box.

"Come out Chrissie. You can help me sort this out."

She immediately heads to the front door of the house. Chrissie, the driver and another removal man follow. She presses the bell, a middle aged attractive man opens the door.

"I suppose my sister told you we arrived," says Maureen.

The man looks around in amazement and notices the van.

"What's up?"

"That's our van."

"A van? What for? Your sister said it was only a few small items?"

Maureen promptly enters the corridor before the man can prevent her.

The removers follow. Chrissie hesitates.

"Whoa! Whoa! Stop," says the man.

In the living room the removal men bring out the antique chest. Maureen stands before a wall with books and the empty box on the floor. She takes a piece of paper out of her pocket with book titles about art and architecture. She browses the book titles. She takes out two heavy books.

"Can you help me Chrissie?"

She gives the books to Chrissie. Chrissie arranges the books in a box on the floor. The man stands and watches her moves with suspicion. They continue taking out and arranging books in the box.

"Chrissie why don't you go to the bedroom, she left some clothes."

Chrissie doesn't react. She makes a move to Chrissie.

"Up, up you go."

Chrissie heads for the door.

"Wait! I'll get them," says the man.

The man leaves and Chrissie returns. Maureen and Chrissie continue.

The box is plenty of books. Maureen adds a last book. The man arrives. He carries a box full of clothes. He shows two pieces of sexy underwear.

"I can't remember wearing these, so they must belong to her."

"She told me it was a birthday present from you!"

"Oh, well."

The man throws the cloths together into the box.

"When I receive a present from my husband Bob, it's usually jewellery!"

"Really? I didn't know he was into kinky stuff," says the man.

Maureen rolls her eyes.

The removers come in again and she points at an antique armchair.

"Take that one!"

Before the removers can touch the armchair the man responds angrily.

"That's the last item that leaves this house. Or I'll call the police and have you all run in for burglary!"

Later in the night Chrissie and Maureen jump out of the van and head towards the entrance of a bar. They go inside.

CHAPTER SIX

That same moment Terry walks in the streets not far from the London bar. He is dressed casual, modern outfit. He goes over his hair with his hands. He checks his mirror reflection in a shop window. For a few moments he listens to a guitar busker. He throws a coin in his cup in front of him and walks again. An old woman comes out of a night shop. She falls. Terry helps her, together with some other people. They bring a chair from the shop and they help her sit down. Terry picks up her shoe that had fallen off and brings it to her. He stays around a short moment, than he walks on. He arrives at the bar where Chrissie and Maureen went inside. He paces outside for a while. He makes a phone call. No answer. He tries again without result. He puts away the phone. He goes in.

Inside the bar Chrissie and Maureen sit on a bar stool. There is loud music. Several empty glasses stand at the bar table. Two men stand at the counter next to them. They cheer. Terry enters the bar and sits at the other side of the counter. He has not noticed Chrissie and Maureen. A woman sitting next him chats to him. They chat and try to make each other understandable within that loud environment. They laugh. All at once some glasses fall with a bang at the counter because Chrissie makes a wrong move. She is drunk. All patrons look in her direction and Terry notices Chrissie and Maureen with male companion and drunk state. He sits frozen and cannot keep his attention on the woman next to him, chatting to him. The woman chats to another man. Terry finishes his drink. He goes outside.

He waits at the door of the bar until a taxi is due and proceeds to the driver.

"Can you take us to Camden?"

"Of course."

"Wait a moment please. I'll get my friend."

He goes inside the bar again and heads to the other side of the counter. Chrissie looks up. He puts Chrissie's glass aside and helps her on her feet. She leans on him. Maureen touches his arm and laughs. He picks up Chrissie's handbag and they head towards the door. Chrissie looks back and waves at Maureen and the two gentlemen. They wave back.

The next morning Chrissie sits at Terry's breakfast table on a bar stool. She holds her head in her hands.

She wears the same clothes as the night before and she looks dishevelled. Terry walks in, dressed for the office. He looks at Chrissie. He goes to a wardrobe. He takes out some medicine and puts it next to her cup of coffee.

"Drink this. It will make you feel sparkier. Maybe you should have some more rest."

"Not possible. I have a presentation at eleven."

"It's all a misunderstanding Terry. Jake is just my business partner, who is coincidentally also a very old friend," continues Chrissie.

"I have to dash. We'll talk later," answers Terry.

In the adjacent street of Phoebe's boarding school, Joe and Rick stand next to a motorbike. They both wear helmets. They keep an eye on Phoebe who is with Claudia and the group of twelve girls and eight boys, gathered at the gates. All fourteen years old. They all wear a blue school uniform and blue rucksack. They look up at a coach that arrives and stops just before the gates of the boarding school. All the youngsters walks towards the coach chatting with each other.

"Look at that. Must be one of those school trips," says Rick.

"It's an opportunity for us," answers Joe.

All the girls have boarded the coach. One of the two female middle aged teachers closes the gates. The two teachers also board the coach. The coach leaves. Joe climbs on the motorbike.

"Let's find out where they are heading to," says Joe.

Rick climbs at the back of the motorbike. The bike follows the coach.

They are arrived in a village. Joe and Rick still follow the coach from a distance. The bus stops at the market place of a small village. Joe and Rick stop behind the church. They park the motorbike and take off their helmets. Rick cleans his face with a handkerchief.

"Luck is on our side. It's only a few miles from our place," says Joe.

The youngsters spread around the village and some take out a sketch book. Phoebe is surrounded by Claudia and two other girls who walk away in the direction of surrounding fields.

"It's seems to be an art excursion," says Rick.

In the surrounding fields of the village, Rick rides around in circles with a boarding school girl on the motorbike. Phoebe, Claudia and one other girl sit against a hedge and draw the landscape. Rick makes a turn and comes close. He stops.

"Somebody else," asks Rick.

"No thanks."

"It's great fun Phoebe," says the girl still on the motorbike.

"I need to finish this," answers Phoebe.

"Lovely drawing," says Rick.

"Thank you," says Phoebe.

"Let's go for another round," says the girl.

She points in the opposite direction.

"That way! The teacher may not find out."

Rick starts the bike and they leave.

Joe stands before the door of the village pub with a glass of beer. The two teachers sit at a small table with a cup of coffee.

"Yeah we could help with a Christmas theme drawing session. Think reindeer and father Christmas on a carriage," explains Joe.

"Do you have a card with your number," asks one of the teachers.

"Ha ha. We aren't sophisticated self-promotors where we are from. You can take my mobile number, now," answers Joe.

Terry sharply takes a Ciabatta sandwich out of the fridge of the coffee house near Russel Square and goes to the counter. He puts the Ciabatta on the counter and talks to the same waitress.

"Hi. You're on duty again?"

"Yeah. How are you?"

"Been very busy lately. Could you please heat that up? And a black Americano."

Terry sits near the window of the coffee shop. He has finished his meal and reads a paper, he turns the page and looks up. He sees Chrissie. He stands sharply. He takes his paper and leaves fast.

In the street he runs after Chrissie.

"Chrissie! Chrissie!"

He waves and Chrissie sees him. She comes towards him.

"Do you have time for a drink?"

"I'd like to but I can't. I have an appointment with an agency and am on my way there."

"That's a pity. We have to talk."

"You know what? Let's walk together."

"Okay, fine."

Terry and Chrissie walk in Russell Square Park. There is an exhibition of owls and one eagle. The birds sit on a perch and are attached to it with a cord.

"Phoebe vaguely remembers that country house of her father and grandfather. I really don't know if it is good or not to explain her more," says Chrissie.

They walk past the birds. An attendant talks to a few people a bit further.

"It's amazing the birds, here in the centre of the city with all these people around," continues Chrissie.

Chrissie walks close by the birds.

"Don't come close. Watch out," says Terry.

The eagle flies all at once from the perch towards Chrissie's head. She flees to avoid the eagle. It's a near miss. Terry runs towards her and embraces her.

"Are you hurt?"

"The bird almost touched my head."

"These are wild animals!"

Terry caresses her head and he kisses her lips. They kiss.

The next day Terry is at work. He walks around in the lab and stops at a chemical construction. His colleague-friend Bob, enters. They both wear a white coat. Bob checks some chemical tubes.

"Terry don't forget the squash game tonight."

Terry stops working and looks up.

"Won't forget. Have to nurture the competitive side of my brain. Isn't that what you mean?"

"Exactly."

"I really have to finish this analysis first," says Terry.

That evening Terry and Bob are finishing a squash game. Bob smashes the ball and wins the game.

"Got you!"

"That's the end of my game. I'm playing bad lately."

In the gym bar Terry and Bob sit at the bar casually dressed. There are a few other people similarly dressed sitting around, some with sporty outfits. A female waiter works behind the till. Terry sits pensively and Bob nervously looks at his iPad. Steve comes in and notices Terry. He notices Terry and ticks on his shoulder. Terry looks up.

"Hi Terry!"

"Steve! Have a seat."

Steve sits next Terry. The waiter stands before him. Bob gets a message on his phone and stands.

"Sorry I have to dash."

Bob shakes hands with Steve and Terry and leaves.

"See you tomorrow Bob," says Terry.

"A scotch please," says Steve.

"Same, me too."

"Good to see you. How are you," asks Steve.

"Not bad, not bad. It's a bit of a roller coaster at the moment relationship wise."

"Why is that?"

"Maybe you are godsend. I'm looking for a flat in the docklands. A good rental. I haven't much time and I want to sort out my accommodation. Chrissie has her own headaches."

Steve offers his hand and they shake hands.

"Deal! You won't get anyone to match my knowledge and skills to assist you," explains Steve.

The waiter brings the drinks. They cheer.

"I am expanding my own portfolio of property investments and I will consider quitting that company," continues Steve.

"Really?"

"Chrissie might have told you?"

"She didn't. She does not talk a lot about work. It's important that we have enough quality time together apart from all work related issues."

"I see. What kind of flat are you looking for?"

"Some new build not too far from Chrissie. It's convenient for her

197

daughter."

"I know about a few interesting new developments in that area. I can arrange a viewing."

"Thanks. I would like to see what's on the market."

The next day at the investment company Steve enters Chrissie's office and sees Chrissie's laptop is unprotected. He sits at her desk. He browses the files. He stops at a file: "Building companies we never invest in".

"Just as I thought."

He browses more and find an "expenses" file. He takes his memory stick from his shirt pocket and uploads both files to the stick. Once this is completed, he stands and closes the window of Chrissie's computer. Steve walks around the room and frantically browses the paper files on her desk. Steve looks around the room.

In the hallway of the investment company Chrissie walks with files. She is just about to enter her office but sees Steve rapidly flicking through the files on her desk. She halts. She tips towards the office door, so that she can spy on Steve. Chrissie hides a bit. Steve continues flicking through the files on her desk.

Steve heads for the doorway of Chrissie's office. Chrissie enters her office. Steve stops and looks up at Chrissie horrified. Chrissie talks in a sarcastic manner.

"Did you find what you are looking for?"

Steve immediately changes his attitude and shows confidence.

"I lost my keys. I've been searching everywhere."

A few evenings later Steve sits opposite a senior manager in an impressive office.

"Look everybody wants to buy some extravaganza. Nothing is wrong with having a strong appetite to make money," explains Steve.

"You cannot borrow with somebody's credit. You have fifteen minutes to gather your personal belongings."

The manager looks at his watch.

"Starting this moment. You are fortunate that we are not going to take legal proceedings against you."

Steve stands.

"I wasn't intending to stay much longer here anyway."

Steve leaves the office.

Chrissie sits at her desk. She works on the computer. She sees Steve walking in the hallway with a box. She hears the front door close with a bang. She continues working on the computer.

Steve and a middle-aged agent sit at the desk of a large modern Docklands office, the office of a letting agent. The agent scrolls the files on his tablet. All similar styled new build Docklands flats pop up.

"We have four similar new build flats. But this one here might be the one for you."

The agent turns the tablet screen towards Steve.

"Right. My client is desperate. So he won't be too fussed if there are no schools, shops or there is no underground station nearby," says Steve.

"I understand. In the end you always find the right person for every flat."

The agent shows several screen views of the flat.

"Actually this is a new build flat with four consecutive price reductions. There are some small building flaws as I told you, but nothing that can't be rectified," continues the agent.

"I need to hire some people to rectify that. Paint work needed also," says Steve.

CHAPTER SEVEN

Steve walks around in Terry's new flat to be. Joe paints white paint on a wall with a brush. Rick paints the other side. A bucket and some gear on the floor in the empty flat. Joe looks around and the at the London skyline.

"What a view!"

He continues painting.

"We might bring in some features of the countryside," says Joe.

"What's the point of that? It will be Terry and Chrissie's flat, not yours," says Steve.

"If my grandchild Phoebe comes here a lot, she must feel as at home."

"Oh, now I understand! But only white walls needed for now. Terry has to sign the contract first," explains Steve.

Rick looks at the walls.

"We could do a projection of virtual reality on these white walls. No need to bring in genuine features of the country," says Rick.

"Yeah, only temporary features needed. By Christmas Phoebe will be back home, where she belongs. She will have a brand new kitchen there also," explains Joe. Steve opens a drawer and picks up the sink tube which had fallen off.

"Don't forget to fix this kitchen unit here."

"No worries. I'll make a note of it," says Joe.

Steve takes up a cloth and wipes away the water on the floor in the corner.

"Water from the ceiling leaks!"

"Each time it rains the leaks will show," says Joe.

"Not a concern for this week as the weather forecast is dry conditions. By that time Terry would have signed the contract. I count on you Joe for showing Terry around," says Steve.

"I can't wait acting as a letting agent," says Joe.

"Not sure you are skilled enough for that," says Rick.

"I can't do it myself. I'm abroad later this week," explains Steve.

Rick enters the door of the living room in the country house, followed by Joe. They carry in between them a large new wood kitchen unit, with sink and cupboard. Rick walks towards the middle of the room.

"Ho ho! Stop that! Stop!"

Rick goes even farther.

"Put that down now!"

Rick lets the cupboard fall with a suddenness.

"Careful!"

"Shut up! It is only a sink."

Joe puts his side carefully on the floor.

"It's not just a sink. It's the sink that your daughter and my granddaughter will use."

Rick wipes the sweat from his face with his arm.

"I won't hold my breath. Wondering will we ever succeed bringing her here."

"Don't be doubting yourself. What I've taught you all our life couldn't have been a total waste of time."

The living room in the country house is nicely lit up by some lamps of modern design. The radio blurts some rock music. Rick cleans the newly installed sink units. Joe enters the door towards the bedrooms. He is dressed up for the city. Rick stops cleaning and looks up.

"What's up?"

Joe puts off the radio.

"Now we can understand properly without that blurring. Put that cloth away and go outside."

"Why is that? Why should I go outside?"

"Just do as I told you."

Rick throws the cloth in the sink and heads towards the door leading to the bedrooms.

"Not that door, stupid. The front door."

"How can I know!"

Rick heads for the door leading towards the courtyard. He opens the door.

"Once outside you close the door and then knock on the door."

"Why?"

"You'll see."

Rick leaves the room and closes the door. He turns and looks inside. He makes some gestures with his face. Joe makes a knocking gesture with his hand.

"Knock on the door."

In the courtyard Rick holds his hand behind his ear and pretends he does not understand what is expected from him to do. Joe repeats the knocking gesture.

"Knock! Just knock!"

Rick looks up and nods. He knocks at the door. Joe heads towards the door, opens the door and makes an exaggerated gesture towards Rick.

"Do come inside sir. I was expecting you."

"Did you?"

"I assume you came for this superb show flat."

"No, I'm just doing as I am told."

Joe makes annoying grimaces.

"Don't lose your act," says Joe.

"I don't understand why I should act in the first place."

"Just do your old man a favour."

Joe regains his act and walk towards the table.

"Let me first thank you for your interest in our company. You couldn't have made a better decision than by choosing us. Life is too short and money is too precious to make bad calls," says Joe.

"Agree! Now can you make it a bit shorter. I have work to get on with."

"Time won't be wasted when we start to see the gains from this prestigious project," continues Joe.

"If you say so."

It's evening and Joe, dressed as a letting agent walks around with Terry in the new flat. The flat is new, looks smart but Joe puts himself before a damp spot. Terry has seen it and looks behind his back.

"Are you hiding something there?"

"Me hiding something? No."

"Isn't that a damp spot?"

"Damp? Are you smelling any damp?"

"No, but."

"They are working at the external wall, it has rained a lot these days. I'll check that later."

"Of course."

Terry writes on his note book.

"No need to write that down."

"How long is this flat for rent?"

"I guess a month or so. Why do you want to know?"

"That's a long time for central London isn't it?"

"Count yourself lucky that we found you something so fast at short notice."

They walk past another damp spot and Joe hides this from Terry's view, distracting him with the outside view.

"Look at the view outside!"

"I can't get enough of looking at it with all these lights," says Terry.

They enter the open plan kitchen area.

"Lovely kitchen," continues Terry.

Terry opens the oven.

"You might cook a good meal in here for the whole family."

"We tend to eat out a lot apart from the odd home delivery."

Suddenly they hear a lot of noise coming from the flat next them.

"What's that noise?"

"Probably the cleaners of the flat next door."

"That's loud!"

Joe bounces on the wall with the side of his fist.

"Shut up there!"

Joe searches through his papers

"You could move in immediately after signing the contract."

"I want to talk to Steve first. I had expected him to be here."

"Something urgent came up. He sent me instead."

Once outside the new building Joe and Terry walk towards Terry's car. It's dark and desolate out. There are older flats next door, not well maintained. Terry opens the door and gets in.

"Where is the nearest tube?"

Joe points in a direction.

"It's a bus stop. Over there you see the bus stationery."

"Really? Thanks for showing me around. I'm off."

Terry slams the door and starts the engine. The car leaves. Joe walks back. A mum with a buggy and followed by three young children pass by. The mum and children are dressed in a poor state, their general appearance is dirty. A motorbike arrives with a man and a girl. The girl jumps from the bike takes off the helmet and slashes the helmet on the man's back in fury.

"You bastard, why did you drive that fast, risk our lives."

Later that evening Joe walks around in the cellar of the building with a rucksack and checks elevator and dead space areas. He pushes a few buttons on a board. He follows the light signals on the buttons of the lift going up and down. He notices a signal for the twentieth floor popping up. He focuses his attention. Joe arrives at the communal bins and empties a rucksack in the large bin for rubbish, on top of the other waste in bin bags. Three pairs of women shoes, two pair with high heels and one pair of pumps fall out.

The following evening the room in the empty flat next to Terry's new flat is lit with a workman's light. Joe stands on the rungs of a ladder and bores a hole in the wall. He holds his eyes before the hole and looks through the hole. He continues until the hole is pierced through and is wide enough. Joe looks through the hole. He steps down from the ladder. He walks around and looks outside the window and notices Terry and Chrissie heading towards the entrance of the building downstairs. He sees Chrissie pointing upstairs and he withdraws from the window.

The lift doors open in the hallway of Terry's new flat. Chrissie and Terry walk out. Terry pushes the light switch in the hallway and looks around.

"Here it is."

Terry takes the keys and they enter. He holds Chrissie close.

Joe stands on the ladder and spies on Terry and Chrissie through the hole in the empty flat next Terry's new flat.

Terry enters his new flat with his back first. Chrissie hangs around his neck. The door closes with a bang.

"Take care with the door!"

They are laughing. They kiss each other. Chrissie withdraws from Terry and they stand hand in hand. They go over to the window and take in the breathtaking view.

"Fantastic, isn't it?"

"Indeed. I'm not sure about the neighbourhood though," says Chrissie.

"I signed the contract already."

"A little hasty. Don't you think?"

Terry starts kissing her again. Terry pushes her on the ground while kissing her. They caress each other and giggle.

Joe stands before the door of Terry's new flat in the hallway and listens to the noises inside with cupped fists, listening to the giggles.

Inside the new flat suddenly Chrissie's phone rings. She grabs her phone.

"Hello? Yes. I understand. I'll be there."

Chrissie tries to stand tentatively. Terry obstructs her.

"I'm sorry about this. I have to dash."

"Chrissie! Let's finish this first."

Chrissie succeeds standing and heads for the door.

"Sorry, says Chrissie."

In the hallway Chrissie heads for the lift. Joe hides behind the corner. She pushes the button. Chrissie enters the lift. The doors almost close. Joe puts his foot between the gap in the door. Chrissie has not seen this and pushes again a button for closing the door. Joe withdraws his foot and the door closes.

A few days later Terry and Chrissie stand in the living room of the new flat. Packages are in the middle of the room. They both sit opposite each other on spare odd chairs. In the corner there is a continuous leak of water from the ceiling where it had been damp water.

"I still not understand why you didn't ask me to look for a flat for you and cast my eye of expertise over it," says Chrissie.

"I'm devastated, we just move and find this! I call Steve."

"Steve? Why Steve?"

"He arranged the rental."

"My god Steve! Are you serious about this? Why did you ask Steve?"

"I met him in the gym and he offered to help me."

"He was fired because of fraud."

"Oh shit! How could I've known this?"

CHAPTER EIGHT

In the middle of the night Joe tries to open the door of a side building next to a farm. He uses an iron stick and tries to force the door open. Rick oversees the farm site.

"You said we could lease the livestock from the farmer! Now you are breaking in," says Rick.

"Shut up! Don't sweat over the small stuff."

"It's not some trivial detail, it's a biggie. There is no way I want to get banged-up in gaol like you did!"

The door gives in. Joe throws the large door open and they find four reindeer in stable, next to two carriages.

"As I expected, their here! We bring them back the day after. Nobody will notice," says Joe.

They walk into the garage stable.

Outside the farm Joe sits on front of a carriage and Joe sits on another. They ride away with the carriages, each with two reindeer attached.

The living room of Terry's new flat is nicely furnished with modern and stylish furniture. The lights are on. An empty bucket sits in the corner of the room directly under the point of an earlier leak. Phoebe sits on the couch before the television watching a teen music program.

"Are you going to stay alone here darling," asks Chrissie.

"I want to watch this programme. Don't worry about me," says Phoebe.

"Well, aren't we going to buy some food so we celebrate Terry's new home, all three of us?"

"Great idea. I'm starved," says Phoebe.

"Don't go outside. A lot of properties are vacant and that means there aren't regular people around, so take extra care!"

"Mum, turn off the light, please."

Chrissie pushes the light switch off. Terry and Chrissie leave. Phoebe watches the teen program. She puts the sounds a bit louder. A projection, with a pulsating light, appears on the wall and overtakes the television screen view. It's the courtyard of Joe's and Rick's country house with snow, four reindeers, outdoor Christmas rope lights and laser lights. Phoebe looks up at the flashing light. Reindeers appear on the wall and overlay on the TV picture. Phoebe rises from her chair.

"What?"

The image disappears. Phoebe looks around bewildered. She sinks back into her armchair. The image appears again. Phoebe looks up. The image disappears. She rubs her eyes. No images anymore now. She relaxes. She watches the teen television music program.

Early morning a coach arrives in the village snowed under. He parks next to the church. Phoebe and Claudia are with the group of twelve boarding school girls and eight boys warmly dressed descend with snow boots. All are fourteen years old. They head across the road for the two waiting carriages each with two reindeer. They stroke the animals. Joe and Rick disguised as Santa's leave the pub. Rick heads for the reindeer and unties the leash of one of the carriages. The female middle aged teacher walks towards Joe. They shake hands.

"The carriages are waiting for you. Ready to discover the landscape," says Joe.

The youngsters climb into the two carriages. The bus driver closes off the coach and heads for the pub.

"Fantastic landscape with the snow covered hills and vales," says the teacher.

"We have a white Christmas season this year," says Joe.

"They will make great drawings today," says the teacher.

The teacher climbs into one of the carriages. Rick climbs on to the front seat of this carriage. Joe unties the leash of the other carriage and takes place on the front seat.

Several youngsters sit against the wood cabin, the hovel of Joe in the middle of the fields, with sketch books. Three boys walk around the fields exploring the surroundings with the teacher. Joe feeds the reindeers of the two carriages. A boy finds a black shoe with high heels. He takes it up and walks towards the hovel.

"Look what I found!"

They all look up.

"Ha ha! Someone must have lost it," says Joe.

The boy lays the shoe against the wall of the hovel and sits down. Rick goes around with cups and a can of hot chocolate. He hands over a cup to Phoebe.

"There. One for you."

Phoebe takes carefully the cup.

"Thanks."

Phoebe drinks the hot chocolate. Claudia lays her sketch book on the floor. She stands with her drink and heads for the door of the wood cabin.

"Freezing cold!"

She disappears inside. Phoebe follows her lead and disappears inside with her cup and sketch book.

The door is ajar and three boys and five girls stand inside the cabin before a small fire in the middle. Phoebe is one of them. A few pieces of small wood lie in the middle of a large iron pot. Rick strums a Christmas song from his guitar. They all sing together.

"Merry Christmas. Merry Christmas to you!"

Joe pops in and throws two more pieces of wood on the makeshift burner. Splashes of fire pop up. The pupils withdraw. Joe drops a pill quickly into the cup of Phoebe and the cup of her girlfriend Claudia. The girls giggle a lot.

Phoebe's sketchbook falls on the floor. Joe pushes it towards a corner of the cabin under some hay. The teacher comes in. She yells at the girls.

"We have to go. It gets dark early this time of the year."

"Sure does! Rick stop that noise," says Joe.

Rick puts his guitar in the corner.

"Blimey! That went smoothly," says Rick.

Outside in the fields everyone has boarded the two carriages. They all karaoke out loud a Christmas song that comes from an ipod in the first carriage.

"Merry, merry Christmas!"

The first carriage with Rick, the teacher, all the boys and two girls takes off. Joe takes up the leash of the second carriage. Phoebe and her girlfriend sit on the second and last carriage with eight other girls. They all sing.

It's dusk. The village street lights illuminate the country. The girls on the second carriage with Joe sing Christmas songs and cheer. Suddenly Phoebe looks on the seat.

"Where is my sketchbook?"

She grabs the book of her girlfriend Claudia.

"That's mine," says Claudia.

"Where is mine? Stop! Stop!"

Joe instructs the reindeers and they stop all of a sudden. The girls bend over and fall on each other and laugh.

"What's up," asks Joe.

"I lost my sketchbook!"

The first carriage disappears inside the village. Joe turns the carriages into the opposite direction. The girls fall over again.

"Ouch!"

"What are you doing," asks Claudia.

"I saw your sketchbook fall off. It flew away. We'll go back and pick it up. It's not far," says Joe.

The carriage moves into the opposite direction.

"Wait! We can walk towards the village," says one of the girls.

He halts the carriage. The eight girls descend the carriage.

"I'll go with Phoebe," says Claudia.

The carriage leaves again with a jolt. The girls walk arm in arm towards the village, opposite direction, singing loud in the darkening fields.

"Where did you see my book fall off," asks Phoebe.

"It's not far. I'm sure that was your book," says Joe.

Joe accelerates with speed and the girls both grip the wood handle to avoid falling out of the carriage. Phoebe scans the floor of the field.

"I can't see anything."

"It was near the cabin."

"The cabin? That's too far. It's getting dark. Let's go to the village."

Joe sets an ever faster pace.

"Stop and slow down! Please let us go," says Claudia.

"Ooh! He's not going to stop," says Phoebe.

Joe doesn't react at all. Claudia climbs towards the front seat.

"I will help him a bit changing his mind."

"No! Don't! Come back! It's too dangerous."

Claudia attempts to force Joe to change direction, without result.

"Come back!"

Claudia falls from the carriage and rolls on the floor. Phoebe follows with her eyes her girlfriend.

"Stop! Stop! She fell off."

Joe does not react. Phoebe still watches her girlfriend Claudia laying for dead on the fields.

"Stop for God's sake! We have to see if she's alright."

In the village Rick stops the carriage and reindeers before the coach. They all jump off.

"Thanks for everything," says the teacher.

"Thanks a lot. We'll come back here," says one of the boys.

"Okay guys. Have a safe trip back to London," says Rick.

The others wave Rick goodbye before entering the pub. Rick waves back.

"Bye!"

Rick manages the rein and leaves immediately.

The group of youngsters who left Joe's carriage and who left Chrissie and Claudia behind, arrive at the pub. They clean their snow boots and they go inside.

CHAPTER NINE

Back in the fields Phoebe sits dumbfounded at the back of the carriage. She grips the woods in relief for having provided security in the carriage. Joe wipes the leash on the two animals.

"Huu!"

Phoebe screams each time that the leash comes down on them.

"Stop! You said my book is in the cabin. There is the cabin!"

She points in the direction of the cabin-hovel. Joe whips more and the reindeer run faster.

"Where did you take me? The village is in the opposite direction!"

"Ha ha! I'll take you to a better place than the village."

"You can't. I have to go back to the coach and boarding school."

"The country is where you belong."

In the coach the driver sits before the steering wheel. The teacher counts the pupils.

"Not everybody's back yet."

"Ho! Where is Phoebe," asks one of the girls.

"Exactly. Phoebe is not present. I'll pop back in the pub to check."

"She can't be there," says another girl.

"Why is that," asks the teacher.

"Because I was the last one who left the pub."

"Oooh! Phoebe and Claudia went back. They didn't arrive yet," says another girl.

"They went back? Where to?" asks the teacher.

"Oooh! Phoebe lost her sketchbook. We jumped off and walked to the village the last half mile," explains one of the girls.

That same evening, in Terry's flat, the doorbell sounds. Terry runs in the dark room naked and half wet with a dark green towel, towards the intercom. He notices Chrissie and pushes the button of the intercom. He dries his body and hair with the towel. Another buzz and he opens the front door. Chrissie steps in. They kiss.

"You smell fresh," says Chrissie.

Terry holds here close.

"Stop. We're late already," continues Chrissie.

"Okay, okay. I'll dress first. Want some coffee?"

He points at the coffee machine in the open plan kitchen.

"Thanks. Hurry up."

Terry leaves the room. Chrissie goes to the coffee machine and puts in a unit. She waits while the coffee cup fills. Suddenly there is a pulsating light from behind the kitchen items on the wall. The picture has formed again on the opposite wall of the courtyard of Joe and Rick's country home, with snow, reindeers, outdoor Christmas rope lights and laser lights. Chrissie looks behind but the light and projection has disappeared. She turns and takes up the cup. There is another flashing light. She turns again. Now she can see the projected image. Chrissie loses hold of her cup.

"Aargh!"

She stands frozen. The image disappears. Terry, dressed formally bar a tie, rushes in. He notices the splash of coffee on the floor and takes a spare cloth from a cupboard underneath the sink.

"What's up?"

He picks up the broken pieces of cup. He wipes the floor.

"Why did you do that?"

Another projection on the wall. Chrissie points at it.

"Look!"

Terry watches speechless. He puts the cloth aside and looks around. The image is gone again.

"Where does that come from?"

He looks at the kitchen wall opposite the projection. He knocks on the wall. The image pops up again.

"Something weird is going on!"

"It's the house of Joe and Rick," says Chrissie.

He locates a small hole in the wall and places his finger over the gap, blocking the beam of light.

"It must come from the neighbouring flat."

Terry takes his finger out and watches the same image again. The image disappears.

"Very bizarre," continues Terry.

"Phoebe!"

"What Phoebe," asks Terry.

"She is in the country today on a school excursion. Phoebe mentioned "reindeer". That image we saw a moment ago was Joe's house!"

"God almighty! Let's look at the flat next door."

He opens the door and Chrissie follows him outside the flat.

The flat next door is totally empty except cleaning and paint stuff. Sitting on several stacked crates is a projector with lights flickering on and off in one second intervals. Terry pushes the door open and walks inside, followed by Chrissie.

"They left the door open," says Terry.

Terry inspects the projector. It's blocked. He unplugs the device and the flashing light stops.

"This is bad. They did that on purpose. Joe and or Rick must be behind this," says Chrissie.

A signal on Chrissie's mobile. She takes her mobile out of her pocket.

"Hello."

"Yes it's me."

Chrissie sits down on the floor against a wall.

"What happened?"

Chrissie turns pale. Terry sits down next her and touches her arm gently.

"We're on our way now," says Chrissie.

The courtyard of the country house is illuminated by Christmas led rope lights, Santa Winter Wonderland lights. Acrylic Santas and snowmen with led lights. Santas in chimneys with led lights. Also Christmas neon effect reindeer and angel rope lights. The outdoor laser lights are switched off. Joe rides the carriage with Phoebe inside. He halts suddenly and immediately jumps off. Phoebe climbs down fast from the carriage and sprints towards the open gate. Joe grabs her arm.

"Ho ho. Not that way darling. Not so quick, my sweetheart. A very warm welcome awaits you inside."

Phoebe yells loudly.

"Not gonna happen!"

He drags her towards the house door.

"Shut up. I'm your grandfather."

"That's a lie!"

"Your mother did not inform you well."

"Liar! Bastard!"

Phoebe hits Joe with her fists and kicks with both legs when juggling her body weight and balance. It doesn't help. Joe opens the door and drags her inside the house. He closes off the door. Phoebe slams her body into the door. She tries to crash the window open whilst furiously screaming at Joe. But the window is firmly shut.

"Let me out, you bastard!"

Three police cars are parked next to the village church. Terry's car arrives and parks. Terry and Chrissie jump out from the back of the car. They run towards the pub.

The living room of the country house is illuminated by the Christmas lights from the courtyard. Phoebe stares at the photos on the wall of herself, as a four year old and the picture of herself in the boarding school playground, at the opposite wall. Suddenly Joe comes in and he closes off the front door of the room immediately. He activates the Christmas lights and tree. He checks the roast cooking in the oven with an automatic clock of the brand new kitchen.

"The roast will be timed-ready, thanks to the installation of digital tech gadgets."

He takes off his coat.

"It's warm inside," continues Joe.

Phoebe watches his moves. He takes up a thermos and a cup. On the bottom of the cup lie several pills.

"Some hot cocoa will do you good."

He pours the hot cocoa in the cup and puts it on the table.

"Who are you? How come you have these pictures?"

"As I told you, you are my granddaughter."

Phoebe watches him with open mouth.

"Take a chair and relax yourself. Your dad will be back shortly."

Phoebe sits at the table before the cup of cocoa. She takes a sip of the cocoa to swallow. She shivers.

"I'll show you your room later."

"My room? I'm not staying. I want to go home."

"We have prepared a pre-Christmas party for you. We will all dress up for that occasion."

Joe walks around and prepares the table for dinner. Phoebe takes from time to time a sip of the cocoa to swallow. She yawns. She struggles to keep her eyes open. She flops backwards on the chair and falls asleep.

Later that night in the living room of the country house, Rick plays the guitar dressed as a Santa. Phoebe wears a Christmas hat of an elf. She dances with Joe around the Christmas tree half in a trance.

"Now it comes," says Joe.

Joe pushes Phoebe outside. Rick follows.

In the courtyard Rick continuous playing the Christmas tune on the guitar. Phoebe stands still in the snow between the four reindeers who walk loosely around in the courtyard. Joe heads for the workroom. Suddenly distortedly loud Christmas songs blast out soaking the entire courtyard area. The four animals scamper around wildly forcing Phoebe to retreat to safety to avoid getting hurt. The outdoor laser lights switch on and illuminate the courtyard, followed a second later by beams of lasers lights. Phoebe looks upward in horror. Joe comes towards her dancing in a sort of trance. After a while Phoebe copies the dancing moves of the two others. All three dance in circles around the reindeers.

In the adjacent fields of the country house, with an imperative urgency, three police cars and an ambulance, draw up to exterior wall of the house. Music so loud that it is distorted bleats out and above. Blinding lasers lights add to the general sensory chaos. Two police men and one police woman in each car alight from there marked cars. Chrissie and Terry leave one of the first police cars. Two male paramedics stay inside the ambulance. The six male police personnel take crow bars from the boot of one of the cars. The policemen deftly place the crow bars into the gap of the wooden gate to prise it open. The three other police women are holding small firearms pointing at the gate centre. After a third crack with the crow bars the gate snaps open. The police swiftly walk in.

Joe, Rick and Phoebe are completely unaware of the nine police moving sharply in the courtyard. Three of the police grab Joe. He fights but he can't escape. Three others take Rick. Terry holds Chrissie. Phoebe continues to dance trance-like in and around the reindeers. Chrissie runs towards Phoebe followed by Terry and the two paramedics. Phoebe collapses in her arms. The paramedics take care of Phoebe. Terry holds Chrissie.

THE END

Printed in Great Britain
by Amazon